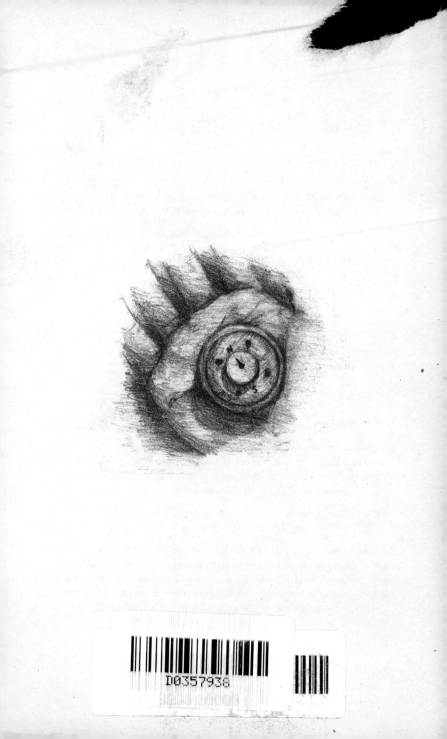

For Callum and Liam Courtney

First published 2010 by Walker Books Ltd
87 Vauxhall Walk, London SE11 5HJ

This edition published 2013

2 4 6 8 10 9 7 5 3 1

Text © 2010 Amanda Mitchison
Illustrations © 2010, 2013 Richard Collingridge

This book has been typeset in Caslon

Printed and bound in Great Britain by Clays Ltd, St Ives plc

British Library Cataloguing in Publication Data: a catalogue record for this book is available from the British Library

Every effort has been made to trace the ownership of all copyrighted material and to secure the necessary permission to reprint the material used in this book. In the event of any question arising as to the use of any material, the publisher, whilst expressing regret for any inadvertent error, will be happy to make the necessary correction in future printings.

ISBN 978-1-4063-4537-7

www.walker.co.uk

MISSIN TELEMARK

AMANDA MITCHISON

FRAGILE

WALKER
BOOKS

21st November 1942

From: Lord Archibald Wetherspoon
              CHIEF OF COMBINED FORCES
To: THE PRIME MINISTER
Subject: OPERATION FRESHMAN

Operation Freshman has failed.
The target was not destroyed. All
servicemen involved are missing in
action. We fear the worst.
We are at a crucial juncture in
this war. The situation becomes ever
more critical. We urgently need an
alternative strategy.

Lord Archibald Wetherspoon
CHIEF OF COMBINED FORCES

21st November 1942

From: THE PRIME MINISTER
To: Lord Archibald Wetherspoon
           CHIEF OF COMBINED FORCES
Subject: OPERATION DRUMMERBOY

We need to use radically different
tactics, and for that I have an unusual
idea. I assume you know that the military
intelligence unit has been training
a group of young teenagers. These
children have been specially selected
through physical aptitude and military
intelligence tests. They are fully
trained troops with unique individual
skills. They are all aged thirteen and
above and all but one come from families
which have sought refuge from the Nazi
regime overseas.

I propose we surprise the enemy and
send in a small band of these children.
They are unlikely to arouse suspicion
and we have nothing to lose now.

PRIME MINISTER

21st November 1942

From: Lord Archibald Wetherspoon
             CHIEF OF COMBINED FORCES

To: Colonel Richard Armstrong
             SPECIAL OPERATIONS EXECUTIVE

Subject: OPERATION DRUMMERBOY

Here are the details of three children – two boys and a girl – selected for Operation Drummerboy. They are due to arrive with you in Scotland shortly. They have completed basic training and have shown great potential in different areas. All are Norwegian nationals and good skiers. They are our best recruits and together they should make an excellent team.

As minors are involved, permissions have been obtained from the highest level. All due consents have also been obtained from parents and guardians.

A third boy, trained by the Norwegian resistance, will join the others next week.

Everything now depends on you. Remember: we have very little time.

Lord Archibald Wetherspoon
CHIEF OF COMBINED FORCES

NAME: ÅSE MILDRED JEFFRIES

DoB: 03.07.28

NATIONALITY: American-Norwegian

LANGUAGES: Bilingual in
Norwegian and English,
fluent German and Spanish

HEIGHT: 1 m 27 cms

WEIGHT: 39 kgs

EYE COLOUR: Brown

HAIR: Black, straight

COMPLEXION: Sallow

DISTINGUISHING FEATURES: N/A

SPECIAL SKILLS: Languages; excellent fine motor skills
— would be suitable for explosives training. Brilliant
gymnast.

- -

Jeffries is a bright girl, barely bigger than a
sixpence. She is physically very agile and what she
lacks in size she more than makes up for in spirit.
Jeffries has trained seriously as a gymnast since
the age of six and won a silver medal in the Junior
category of the 1941 English Gymnastics Championships.
She is neat-fingered and also shows some artistic
ability. So far her life has been peripatetic. Her
American father is in the oil-prospecting business
(a geo-engineer with Shell) and her Norwegian mother
travels with him. The family haven't lived in Norway
for nearly a decade. Åse is currently a boarder at
Roxbury Hall, a special school for gifted gymnasts and
dancers on the South Downs.

Some instructors have raised doubts about Åse's
temperament. She flies off the handle easily and
doesn't tolerate fools gladly. But nobody can beat
her for staying power and guts. Being small could
be a great advantage on some missions.

NAME: FREDERICK ST CLAIR HAUKERD

DoB: 26.05.28

NATIONALITY: Norwegian

LANGUAGES: Bilingual in Norwegian
and English. Due to his immense
academic capability, Frederick
can read many written languages,
notably Latin, Sanskrit, Hebrew,
Arabic and some Aramaic.

HEIGHT: 1 m 63 cms

WEIGHT: 46 kgs

EYE COLOUR: Blue

HAIR: Bright red, wavy

COMPLEXION: Fair, extensive freckles

DISTINGUISHING FEATURES: 5 cm L-shaped scar on right
temple. Wears glasses.

SPECIAL SKILLS: Photographic memory — would be good
in communications and intelligence work

Haukerd has a graduate-level grasp of physics and
biochemistry and can solve complex mathematical
equations with ease. He is widely read, with
surprising pockets of knowledge (alpine plants,
Dresden clocks, medieval music, etc.). He possesses
a photographic memory and can read and reproduce
entire pages of a telephone directory. His main
instructor says he's so clever you could fry an egg
on his forehead. The other children on the course
call him "three-brain Freddie".

Frederick was born in Norway but has lived with
his family in England since 1935 when his parents
emigrated. He comes from a large, eccentric family
(he is the eldest of six children). His mother is a
developmental biologist and his father is a Sanskrit
scholar at the London School of Oriental and African
Studies.

Haukerd can ski well, but is otherwise physically
inept. He's clumsy, accident-prone and sometimes
absent-minded.

NAME: JAKOB P. STROMSHEIM

DoB: 10.12.27

NATIONALITY: Norwegian

LANGUAGES: Norwegian (native language), fluent unaccented English, some French

HEIGHT: 1 m 60 cms
WEIGHT: 50 kgs
EYE COLOUR: Blue

HAIR: Fair, straight

COMPLEXION: Fair

DISTINGUISHING FEATURES: N/A

SPECIAL SKILLS: Very good with people. A born leader and all-round athlete.

- -

Stromsheim is steady, competent, organized and utterly dependable. He has natural authority and is resourceful and wise beyond his years. He has a well-ordered mind and a useful ability to bring out the very best in others. He was a great favourite among his trainers and they believe he has outstanding leadership potential.

This boy has grown up in a hurry. He lived in a coastal village in Norway until his family fled to Britain in April 1940. His father was involved with the Norwegian resistance and undertook missions for MI5 and the Special Operations Executive until he was reported missing in action. Stromsheim is an only child. His mother works in a munitions factory but suffers from fragile mental health. We suspect that young Jakob may be a worrier — but he is never flustered and always remains outwardly calm.

23rd November 1942

From: Colonel Richard Armstrong
            SPECIAL OPERATIONS EXECUTIVE
To: Lord Archibald Wetherspoon
            CHIEF OF COMBINED FORCES
Subject: OPERATION DRUMMERBOY

We have never resorted to using minors before and I have serious reservations about this initiative. We must, however, learn from this experience. We need to know exactly what the children are doing, when and where. We must understand how they react under pressure, how they cope.

To this end, I am giving the children a log book, with instructions to fill it in with as much detail and documentary back-up material as possible. I want everything recorded: not just the weather and their progress, but their thoughts, mishaps, disagreements — everything.

This is a dangerous and important mission. In the not unlikely event that these individuals come to grief, I hope this log will provide reassurance to their families that their lives were not lost in vain. You do not have to remind me what is at stake.

Colonel Richard Armstrong
SPECIAL OPERATIONS EXECUTIVE

Nothing to be written or typed in this margin

Jakob P. Stromsheim

Colonel Armstrong has given me this log book so we can all write up what happens to us. I've read the memos and profiles in the front, and I'm flattered that I'm thought to have "leadership potential" (whatever that means). But I'm not quite so pleased to discover how dangerous the Colonel seems to think this mysterious mission is going to be.

The Colonel says we should try and make a record of events as soon as possible, when everything is still fresh in our minds. But he intends to keep us so busy I'm probably only going to have time to fill in the log in short bursts.

So here goes!

I'm writing this in the library by a huge log fire. There are leather-bound books all round the room. It's warm and cosy – quite a contrast to our terrifying welcome to Drumincraig House and our first encounter with its strange occupants.

The journey from our old training camp in Monmouthshire turned out to be long and chilly. And it wasn't quite over when Åse, Freddie and

I arrived at a tiny deserted railway station in the middle of the Scottish Highlands. I've always fancied that I'm better at drawing than writing, so I've made a little sketch to show you what it was like.

We were standing around outside, hoping someone would come and collect us because it was freezing cold, when suddenly a Bentley came careering down the road towards us. Or rather *at* us. We jumped back from the pavement just in time.

Neeeeeeeeeeeeoooooow!

The Bentley screeched to a stop, sending mud flying everywhere.

A wiry man with a toothbrush moustache and slicked-back hair popped his head out of the window.

"Good day!" he cried. "I'm Sergeant Sneyd! In you get! At the double! Chop-chop-chop!"

Was he mad? Or drunk? Were his pants on fire?

I was only half in the car when he set off so fast it sounded like he was trying to skim the tarmac off the road. I tumbled into my seat and slammed the door. Åse's eyes widened. After two months in the training camp, where there was no talking allowed at mealtimes, we'd all become good lip-readers. *Another lunatic!* she mouthed. And Freddie and I knew immediately what she meant. We've met some pretty strange characters during our time together, but it looked like Sergeant Sneyd could be the worst yet.

He drove like a bat out of hell. *Whoosh!* Up over a mountain pass. *Whoosh, whoosh!* Down a zigzag road. Up another mountain pass and down again. Then more hairpin bends at breakneck speed until suddenly we approached a huge metal gate with stone lions on either side. Sergeant Sneyd swerved the Bentley off the road and we crashed through the gate and along a long, tree-lined drive. When we got to a fork in the drive, the Sergeant brought the car skidding to a halt, fanning mud out everywhere.

"Out now. At the double! Chop-chop-chop! Take your bags round to the front and let yourselves in! Say hello to Bruno from me! Ha-ha!" He barked a laugh, and then, as soon as we'd got our last bag out of the car, he drove off again – making another great fan of mud.

So we were left to trudge up the driveway lugging our bags and gas masks. I thought we'd finished basic training and all those endless endurance exercises, but this felt like another test.

The driveway was long – a couple of kilometres at least – so I had plenty of time to wonder exactly *why* we were here. What *was* this mission we'd been selected for? And why on earth choose us?

As we walked on through the trees we began to catch glimpses of a very large house with clusters of towers and turrets. We passed an ornamental garden with an old broken-down stone fountain and shaggy box hedges. Rabbits were nibbling in the flower beds. The house, its windows dark, rose up in front of us. It was just a little scary.

"Betcha it's haunted," said Åse.

I turned to Freddie. He may have wolfed down all our sandwiches before the train even left Edinburgh, but he has his uses. He's our encyclopaedia on legs. "Got any facts on the house, Freddie?"

Freddie chewed his lip. "Not much. Dates back to 1840. Architect was David Bryce. Scottish baronial style, part of the Victorian gothic revival in architecture. Gargoyle of the Duke of Wellington in the great dining room. Oak panelling. Plumbing added later. Foundation stone laid by—"

"So what you're *really* saying," said Åse, cutting him off, "is that the bathrooms will be miles from the bedrooms and freezing cold."

Freddie nodded. "Yes, and the food will be horrible."

At the front of the house a sweep of wide stone steps led up to an ornate metal porch.

"Come on," I said. "Let's get inside."

In a rush of enthusiasm, I leapt up the steps three at a time, which was a mistake because…

Holy mackerel!

I gasped and took a step back, but it was too late to run away.

There by the door, its eyes glinting in the shadow, stood a huge brown bear.

The bear made no sound. It remained frozen, claws raised, staring fixedly at me. It had that terrible stillness of an animal about to pounce.

I held its gaze. Knowing I had only a moment to make my move, I felt in my pocket for my Swiss Army penknife. I knew that if I threw it and caught the bear just above the eye, it'd be knocked out cold.

I focused my mind on that spot and threw the knife as hard as I could.

Wham!

With a terrible, agonizing *crack!* the creature keeled over and smashed its head open against the balustrade.

Gingerly – almost on tiptoe – we stepped forward towards the great furry mound. There was a hole the size of a man's fist in the bear's skull, and the contents of its brain were trickling out across the stone slabs.

As usual, Åse was the first to break the silence.

"Poor thing," she said in a hushed voice. "It couldn't break its fall."

Freddie looked at the furry mound thoughtfully. "And of course its arms were useless."

I dipped my fingers in the fine powder collecting at the bear's feet. "It's hard to think quickly when your head is stuffed with sawdust."

Then I don't know what came over us … exhaustion, probably. It seemed ridiculous that we'd been taken in by a stuffed bear! We sat down together on the steps and started to laugh.

And this meant that we didn't hear the door opening behind us.

"So you got here at last," said a soft voice with a distinct Scottish accent. We quickly turned round. An enormously tall, bony, slightly stooped man was standing in the doorway. He had a huge, beaky nose and his trousers were hitched up high above his waist.

The man looked us up and down and sucked his teeth. He spoke slowly, looking at each of us in turn. "Stromsheim, Haukerd, Miss Jeffries. I suppose you'd better come in." With the slightest flicker of a smile, he added, "Once you've put Bruno back on his feet again."

The bear turned out to be pretty ancient and moth-eaten. A small plaque on the stand read:

BRUNO 1874-82

After we had resurrected Bruno, the man led us into a large hallway with a stone floor and rows of guns and spears and mounted animal heads fixed to the walls. Cripes! What a place we'd ended up in! There were tigers, wolves, wild boar and lots of antelopes with strange, corkscrew-shaped antlers. I found I was shivering – the hallway was cold, and in a strange trick of the light every single one of these creatures seemed to be looking straight at me.

The man stood looming over us with his hands clasped behind his back.

"Allow me to introduce myself," he said. "My name is Colonel Armstrong. I'm called Dickie by my friends, but I'll be sir to all of you." He lowered his head and looked down at us over the rim of his glasses.

"Welcome to Drumincraig House. From now on you are my charges. I'm afraid you won't find many luxuries here. Don't expect any fluffy towels, or perfumed soap. It's not that kind of place. But you'll soon get used to breaking the ice in your washbasin every morning. As for the food…" Here Colonel Armstrong paused and gave a crooked little smile. "Well, that will be what you make of it.

"There are just a few rules," he continued. "Doors marked NO ENTRY *mean* no entry. Breakfast is at 7.30 sharp. The billiard table is out of bounds – replacing the felt costs a fortune – and anything in a case, or in a drawer, must be left alone."

The Colonel looked at Freddie and me. "Stromsheim and Haukerd, you are in the big room on the first floor immediately facing the stairs. Miss Jeffries, you'll find your bedroom on the top floor. Up the stone staircase, turn left at the stuffed lynx, pass the model of HMS *Great Britain*. If you come to the beetle collection you've gone too far.

"Anyone got any questions? No? Good! You're here to prepare for your mission and we don't have much time. You have five minutes to dress for dinner. No pearls or bow ties here. You'll need hats, coats and gloves. Meet in the dining room at 15.32 precisely. Dismissed!"

Upstairs we saw our bedrooms for the first time. Freddie and I are in a large shabby room with peeling lino on the floor and little steps up to a round turret in one corner. There are three beds – we've been told there'll be another boy joining us soon – and it's absolutely freezing. Freddie's ears and nose looked red as berries. He couldn't have been any colder.

"Freddie, take that bed there. It's next to the basin," I said. "The hot pipe to the taps will run past it."

"But look at the basin," replied Freddie miserably. "There *is* no hot tap."

He was right. There was no hot tap.

Jakob P. Stromsheim

I'm in bed and I've been trying to sleep but my feet are too cold, so I thought I'd write about dinner instead. (Hopefully my feet'll warm up soon.)

At precisely 15.32, as instructed, we were all in the dining room. It looked very grand, but there was no sign of food, no cutlery, no glasses and no smells of cooking. Instead, at each place setting, there was a large, carefully folded dishcloth.

"Take your places!" said Colonel Armstrong.

We sat down.

"Open your dishcloths!"

I opened up the folds. Inside the cloth I found ten lead pellets, a box of matches, a small-ish penknife, a sturdy catapult and a page of instructions on the skinning and gutting of rabbits.

We looked at each other, completely astonished. We each had the same little pile of equipment. Not even Åse had anything to say.

Colonel Armstrong gave us another crooked little smile. "Well, it'll be dark soon, so get a move on. Supper's outside. You're all trained in small arms fire, so it won't take you long to get the hang of those

THIS WEEK'S
FOOD FACTS
PREPARING A RABBIT
FOR COOKING

GUTTING THE RABBIT

1. Hold the rabbit up by the forepaws and squeeze the lower abdomen to empty the bladder.

2. Cut a line in the rabbit's belly from the bottom of the ribcage to the anus. Be careful not to go too deep – if you cut open the stomach or intestines, the meat will be spoiled.

3. Insert middle and forefinger into the cut and scoop out the guts.

4. Check the cavity for any residual pieces. (The kidneys may stay attached to the ribcage, but they should be fine to eat.)

MINISTRY **M** of **F** OF FOOD

SKINNING
THE RABBIT

1. Chop off the paws, head and tail.

2. At the abdominal cut, pull the skin up and separate it from the muscle. Insert your fingers between the two layers and rotate your hand until you have completely separated the skin all round the rabbit's midriff (the skin should come away quite easily).

3. Make a cut along the inner thigh of one back leg and pull the skin away. Remove the skin from the other back leg in the same way.

4. When both back legs are free, grip the skin firmly and with one swift motion pull upwards. The rest of the rabbit pelt should come away in one piece. The rabbit is now ready to be cooked.

PLEASE NOTE
Wild rabbits are prone to many diseases. Before cooking, examine the rabbit's heart and liver. If you find green spots, discard the carcass.

catapults. And you'll need to know how to butcher an animal." (I wonder why we'll need to know this.) "Don't build your fire inside or within four metres of the house."

And then, just as Freddie let out a faint whimper, the Colonel cried, "Bon appetit! Dismissed!"

We trudged outside, feeling thoroughly dejected, and made for the ornamental garden where we'd already seen lots of rabbits. But as well as having lots of rabbits, the ornamental garden also had lots of small box hedges that the rabbits could hide behind. And we had Freddie who – typically – stumbled noisily on a wet branch just as we approached.

That was it! The rabbits ran for cover.

We crouched down behind two rhododendron bushes and waited. Slowly, in dribs and drabs, the rabbits returned to their feeding. But the light was fading and the rabbits kept their distance. I could feel Åse getting fidgety and losing patience. Then she fired at a rabbit over by the fountain, which was too far away. Her shot fell short. In a scurry of white bottoms, the rabbits fled.

"What are we going to do?" asked Freddie in a despairing voice.

"We're going to kill a rabbit," I replied.

"I know that!" hissed Freddie. "But how are we

going to *eat* it? We haven't any mustard. You have to have mustard with rabbit. Maybe we could shoot a pheasant instead. They're so much tastier…"

Åse rolled her eyes.

"I'll see you in a bit," said Freddie. "You shoot the bunny. I'll do the rest."

And before we could call him back, he scuttled off down the path.

Åse and I hunkered down again behind the bushes, catapults at the ready. This time the rabbits took an age to reappear, and when they did come back they were even more cautious than before. Now they grazed in little groups, completely out of range.

It was beginning to get really dark when I suddenly felt a crick in my neck. I turned my head to stretch it out and there it was – a lovely large, plump rabbit on the path just behind me!

In a trice I released the pellet and the rabbit's head jerked to the side. Its legs crumpled under it.

Åse ran over to the creature. "It's not dead!" she said in an appalled voice.

The rabbit was twitching horribly. I picked it up by the back legs, swung it round and thumped its head against a paving stone. It came down harder than I intended, spattering me with blood.

At this point Freddie reappeared, his coat pockets

bulging. When he saw the rabbit, he rubbed his hands together cheerfully. "Aha!" he said. "This'll be my job! Give me a couple of your hair slides, Åse, and I'll do the cooking."

We were only too happy to leave Freddie to prepare the rabbit. And while I cleaned off my bloodstains in the old fountain, Åse gathered up wood to make a fire. Meanwhile Freddie sawed off the rabbit's paws with a penknife and then, with a terrible tearing sound, he tugged the skin off in one piece. He offered Åse one of the paws to keep for good luck and looked a bit puzzled when she shuddered. Then he gutted the animal and prepared it for roasting.

We built a fire in a sheltered spot near to the garden wall and Åse found two Y-shaped sticks and an old piece of metal railing which we used as a spit. Then we huddled round the flames while Freddie slowly turned the rabbit on the spit and tried to stop it falling into the fire every two seconds.

Gradually the rabbit began to sizzle. It smelled *so* good.

"I stuffed it with herbs from the kitchen garden," said Freddie. "Chives and thyme and rosemary." Then he added, a little regretfully, "They're so much thinner without their fur on. Maybe we should've got two."

I looked at the rabbit and then I looked at us. Freddie was right – it was a bit skinny. Åse looked at the rabbit too.

"Hey!" she cried. "Those are my hair slides!"

"Well, I had to use something to keep the stuffing in place," said Freddie.

We went on sitting there getting hungrier and hungrier, and after a while we just couldn't wait any longer. We took the rabbit off the spit, and tore the limbs apart. The meat on the outside burnt our fingers and the flesh was still rather raw in the middle, but we didn't really mind.

There wasn't much rabbit left when Colonel Armstrong appeared suddenly out of the darkness. He stood above us, and the light from the fire made his face look particularly gaunt and beaky.

"Would you like to try some, sir?" asked Åse. "Fred's flavoured it with fresh herbs."

Colonel Armstrong cocked an eyebrow at Freddie.

"Sir," said Freddie, "what's for supper tomorrow night? Will it be rat? Or crow? I've heard squirrel can be very good indeed – a nice, gamey flavour."

The Colonel gave him a grim little smile. "I'm afraid it'll be rabbit again," he said. "But tomorrow you'll have to kill it with your bare hands."

So that was dinner. I'm giving the log over to Åse tomorrow. She says she usually writes a diary, so hopefully she'll be better at describing things. (I've never seen anyone write as fast as her – it's surprising the pen doesn't catch fire!)

Åse Jeffries

25TH NOVEMBER 1942, DRUMINCRAIG HOUSE

I'm writing this in the dining room after breakfast, having spent my first night in Drumincraig House. It *definitely* wins the prize for MOST CREEPY AND UNCOMFORTABLE PLACE IN THE UNIVERSE.

In some ways it's worse – if that's possible – than Roxbury Hall (my horrible boarding school where, apart from schooling me till I drop, they're also intent

on turning me into a Proper English Lady).

Here's how Drumincraig measures up:

1. The bedroom:

Icy cold. A colony of daddy-long-legs dance around the light fitting. Sounds of rats (or vampire bats?) sharpening their nails in the enormous corner cupboard.

2. The bed:

Unspeakable. Cold and clammy, as if previously occupied by some monster of the deep. Lumpy mattress, sheets made of slippery nylon that snags on your toenails. If you move even a fraction in the night all the bedclothes slide to the floor.

3. The bathroom:

Miles away. Turn the tap on and there's a sound like a volcano erupting.

Last night, when we came in from the rabbit hunt, the Colonel sent us down to the kitchen where a nice, fat, smiley woman called Mrs Collins gave us mugs of hot milk and set down a tray of toast and dripping. She wasn't counting the slices (the way the Roxbury Hall matron does) and when I put a spoonful of sugar in the milk she winked at me.

Then I went upstairs, and the bedroom was icy. I just got straight into bed as quickly as possible. Tomorrow night I won't drink anything in the evening – if I want to go for a pee in the night I have to pass the old laird's Madagascar beetle collection.

We still haven't been told what we're doing here. Hopefully we'll find out today. But the best thing so far is that the food – when we're not hunting it ourselves – is *bliss*.

For breakfast we've just had fried kippers and eggs and porridge and as much toast and raspberry jam as we could eat. I thought I'd had a bad night, but it turns out that the pillows on the boys' beds have metal bars in the middle. When Fred complained, Sergeant Chop-chop-chop yelled at him, saying it was only an old orthopaedic pillow and called him "a right lady's blouse" for wanting to swap it. Then, just to get the message across, he gave Fred an almighty slap on the back that sent him careering into a little nest of antlers which the Colonel uses as a stand for his galoshes.

I've got to stop now. Colonel Armstrong has come into the dining room with Sergeant Chop-chop-chop at his heels. The Colonel is carrying a sheath of papers under his arm and has just looked at me over the rim of his spectacles and given me a put-down-that-pen-

and-listen-to-me-right-now nod. What a cheek! It was him who wanted us to write this in the first place!

Åse Jeffries

27TH NOVEMBER 1942, DRUMINCRAIG HOUSE

This morning at breakfast the Colonel handed out our timetables. But it's not like school – they don't have English, maths, history, etcetera. Instead the subjects are:

FITNESS DRILL
EXPLOSIVES OR SIGNALS
CLIMBING
COMBAT
FIRING RANGE
ORIENTEERING
FIRST AID AND SURVIVAL
EXTREME CONDITIONS TRAINING

We *still* don't know what our mission is going to be, but we *have* been divided up. Fred (who will probably master Morse code in a flash) and Jakob are studying signals. I'll be learning explosives with the other boy who's due to arrive soon.

"Sir," Jakob said to Colonel Armstrong, "we did quite a bit of judo in Monmouthshire. What other kinds of combat will we need to learn?"

The Colonel started to count on his long, bony fingers. "Unarmed hand-to-hand, knives, garrottes, a little bit of jujitsu, a spot of karate, pressure points ..." he paused here and out came one of his grisly grins, "and, of course, silent killing."

There was an icy silence as we all absorbed the news that we were going to learn to become murderers.

But the Colonel only shrugged. "Don't worry," he said. "You'll soon get the hang of it, and we only practise on dummies to start with."

Well, that *sure* made me feel better...

And I'm flummoxed. What do they have in mind for us? Why are we learning silent killing? When Pop said I needed an English education, I don't think this is quite what he had in mind.

Anyway, I had my first explosives training session this morning. Then, after an *enormous* lunch, we went down to the stone hall, with all those animal heads a-goggling down on us. The wind was howling down the chimney and outside there was nothing but that crazy Scottish rain that comes in sideways in great gusts.

We stood there hoping Colonel Armstrong was going to say, "Why not take the afternoon off? There's a nice fire in the library. Go and curl up there with a board game and a plate of chocolate biscuits."

But not a bit of it. He looked out the window, chewed on his pipe and said – I wish I could do his accent – "Now for a wee stroll up Ben Mor."

Well… The wind was blowing so hard we could barely get the front door open and we were soaked to the marrow in minutes. The Colonel's legs are hugely long and he walks like a dromedary, with great lolloping strides. I had to do Scouts' pace – ten paces running, ten paces walking – to keep up. I know I'm small, but being anywhere near the Colonel makes me feel the size of a dachshund.

At the foot of the path up Ben Mor – which is, of course, insanely high – there was a small shelter. Here the Colonel deigned to stop. "Miss Jeffries! Haukerd! Stromsheim!" he said. "Pick up your packs!"

I couldn't believe it. In the shelter were three rucksacks filled with rocks. I thought only prisoners in Alcatraz carried rocks, but clearly I'm wrong.

I was barely able to move with my pack, but then Jakob told me to fasten the bottom belt of the rucksack – which meant I took most of the weight on my hips rather than my shoulders. So instead of being unbearably heavy, the rucksack became merely excruciatingly heavy.

Up we trudged. Up and up and up. And up. I'm proud to say I didn't snivel, though I darned well felt like it. I tried to forget that I was cold and soaking wet and that all I was going to have for supper was more of Fred's skinny half-burned, half-raw gourmet bunny.

And what I didn't know was that the Colonel had a little treat in store for us: thirty one-armed press-ups each on the summit!

No doubt tomorrow he'll be pulling out our toenails with red-hot pliers.

We got back to Drumincraig at dusk, completely bushwhacked and pig-whimperingly cold and wet. I knew I had to change out of my wet things but I couldn't bear the thought of that freezing cold bedroom. I wandered downstairs to see if there were any spare legs of roast lamb or apple turnovers floating round the kitchen – at least it's a bit warmer down there – and as I got to the long stone corridor in the basement, I heard a "Psst". A door marked NO ENTRY had opened a fraction and Fred was beckoning me in.

He'd found the boiler room! He'd also managed to filch some custard creams from Mrs Collins. It turns out Fred is a practised thief. He comes from a big, hard-up family and says he'd never had a boiled egg to himself before he started this training.

We sat by the lovely warm boiler eating the biscuits and watching the steam rise off our clothes. And it

Up Ben Mor
by Jakob Stromsheim

was then we heard the voices. Mrs Collins sounded really angry.

"You can't do that, Colonel!" she exclaimed.

Then came some murmuring which must have been Colonel Armstrong, though we could only make out the words "hunting" and "hardening up".

But Mrs Collins' voice was loud and clear. "They're children! And while they're under my care they'll have a nice warm supper and that's the end of it!"

Fred punched the air.

So this evening we didn't have to murder bunnies with our bare hands. Instead, Mrs Collins served us a proper shepherd's pie. Make no mistake, this wasn't horrible wartime Roxbury Hall shepherd's pie made with a tiny bit of mince and lots of grey oatmeal and diced turnip to pad it out. No. This was proper, juicy, meaty shepherd's pie. I'm going to write that again: PROPER, JUICY, MEATY SHEPHERD'S PIE!

I don't know what they're doing about rationing – our cards only entitle us to a slither of bacon every hundred years. When I asked Mrs Collins she said, "There's plenty of sheep fall down ravines here." Then she winked.

Just before I went to bed, Colonel Armstrong gave me this piece of paper with the new boy's "resumé" on it.

I'm really curious to meet him, but I wonder if we're all going to get on. Jakob and Freddie and I have

NAME: LARS PETERSEN

DoB: 02.08.28

NATIONALITY: Norwegian

LANGUAGES: Bilingual in Norwegian and English (educated at the international school, his written Norwegian is poor)

HEIGHT: 1 m 70 cms
WEIGHT: 55 kgs

EYE COLOUR: Blue

HAIR: Blond, straight

COMPLEXION: Fair

DISTINGUISHING FEATURES: N/A

SPECIAL SKILLS: A good outdoorsman and skilled navigator

Petersen has been active in the Norwegian resistance for two years. He has worked as a courier in Oslo for the underground press and also as a guide in mountain regions, helping fugitives escape. He is brave, hardy and physically very fit.

Surviving in the wild comes naturally to Petersen. His family have a holiday hut in the mountains above Oslo and he has accompanied his father on hunting trips from an early age. His uncle was on Amundsen's expedition to the South Pole.

Petersen was recently interrogated by the Gestapo and managed to withstand the ordeal without giving away the names of his contacts or details of his work. The experience has clearly affected him, though he has been unwilling to discuss what happened. Petersen is a complex character — a loner at heart and uncommunicative —but his outdoor survival skills are unsurpassed.

been together for weeks now and, though we have our moments, we're a tight little band of friends. And Lars sounds like a dark horse. (He's practically twice as tall as me! I'll need binoculars to look him in the eye!) And what exactly does "complex character" mean?

I'm in bed now, stuffed with shepherd's pie and completely pooped. I'm sure I'll sleep well if that strange scrabbling sound from the cupboard doesn't keep me awake. But I *am* wondering what the Colonel has in store for us. I know it's a difficult, dangerous mission and probably has something to do with Norway (why else would we all be Norwegian speakers?). But what exactly are we going to do? And *what* is living in my bedroom cupboard?

Jakob P. Stromsheim

28TH NOVEMBER 1942, DRUMINCRAIG HOUSE

I'm snuggled up in a shabby old armchair by the fire in the library. It's my favourite place in Drumincraig. I wish we had a big wood fire like this at home – it would really cheer Mother up.

The final member of our team has arrived.

We were at lunch when Mrs Collins brought him in. He was wearing muddy clothes, and I couldn't see him properly at first because he walked with his head down and his hair flopping over his face. He sat down at the end of the table beside Åse and opposite me.

"Children, this is Lars Petersen," said Mrs Collins soothingly. "That would be 'Paterson' here in Scotland." She set down a plate of Lancashire hotpot in front him. "Lars will sleep in the bed next to yours, Jakob. Colonel Armstrong has asked you to look after him. He's come all the way from Norway and he's had quite a journey."

Well, of course I wanted to ask him about this immediately. He must have been smuggled out, just like I was when the Germans invaded Norway two years ago.

I didn't feel I could ask him straight away, though. Lars hadn't said a word to nice, friendly Mrs Collins and he still hadn't lifted his eyes from the floor.

So I said, "Hello, Lars. My name's Jakob. This is Åse. And this bookworm here—" I gave Freddie a nudge, because he had his nose in the Morse code manual "—is Freddie."

Lars didn't reply. He just picked up his fork and started to eat.

I knew he understood English, but maybe he didn't like talking in his second language. So I tried Norwegian.

Well, darn me! He just continued eating, shovelling the food in as fast as he could.

Then Åse had a go.

"Hi, buddy!" she said. "We've been training this morning. You'll be doing explosives with me. It's a bit like school – you sit at a desk and do the maths to calculate the charges. But making the bombs and moulding the explosive is good fun."

Lars ignored her and carried on eating.

Åse gave me a Look.

I tried again. "You're lucky you're not doing signals like Freddie and me. You have to learn all about transmitters and accumulators and codes. And Morse is a real headache – we're having to listen to hours of little bleeps."

And Lars just continued eating – fork to mouth, fork to mouth, fork to mouth.

I felt like a fool. People who don't talk often have that effect on me. I just hear myself blethering away and I sound so empty and stupid.

We didn't know what to do. Åse kicked Freddie under the table and, at long last, he glanced up from his book. Freddie isn't normally very tuned in to people, but he looked at Lars and seemed to understand. "You can have second helpings," he said. "Just go up to the hatch and ask Mrs Collins."

Immediately Lars sat up and swept his hair back from his face. He was deathly pale and completely covered in scratches. His lip was swollen and I could see stitches to the side of his mouth. A large dark red graze ran all the way from his right cheekbone down to his chin. But that was only the superficial stuff.

It was his eyes that were really shocking.

He'd got the wild, hollow-eyed look you get in cornered animals. He didn't seem to be in the same room as us at all. He was somewhere else, where something unimaginable was passing before his eyes and burning itself deep into his mind.

Then, suddenly, Lars shook his head and seemed to bring himself back to the present. He rose to his feet and walked briskly over to the serving hatch.

"Cripes!" said Åse. "Did someone just step over his grave?"

Jakob P. Stromsheim

I'm sitting by the library fire again – this chair is so comfortable I don't think I'll ever get out of it. But back to today's training...

After lunch Sergeant Sneyd, who seems to get scarier every time I see him, led us out to an old barn in the grounds for our first combat lesson. "I call this my Bluebeard room," he said as he unlocked the door. "Ha-ha-ha!"

And, in the half light, the barn did look very sinister. Hanging from the ceiling were six naked tailors' dummies. They were rather battered and had small Xs drawn on them with an ink pen.

"Right, everyone!" bellowed Sergeant Sneyd – he was in his element – "Look sharp! Shoulders up! Backs straight! Chop-chop-chop!" He looked us up and down contemptuously. "Have any of you done any boxing or wrestling at school?"

Freddie and I nodded.

Sneydy gave a snort and continued, eyes flitting from side to side. "Well you can forget that fancy stuff!

Forget your Japanese strangleholds and your spinal dislocators. And you can also forget about fair play. When it comes to a fight for life and death you've got to go for the vulnerable bits of the body – the eyes, the crotch, the back of the neck, the base of the throat. Today you will learn to kill your enemies outright. Without firearms. This is *war*, not sport.

He narrowed his eyes, raised his hand above his head and swirled it through the air like a cutlass. "This," he said, "is a deadly weapon. If used correctly it can kill, paralyse or break bones. But—" and his hand moved so fast that I couldn't even see it "—speed is of the essence."

After that, Sergeant Sneyd showed us how to flex our hands and where to strike an opponent (hence the little Xs drawn on the dummies), using the base of the hand, which is stronger than the fist. For some moves we had to keep our fingers spread out, ready to jab into an opponent's eyes or mouth. Sergeant Sneyd is a *very* dirty fighter.

We practised the moves in slow motion first, then, once we'd mastered a pattern of a few strokes, we sped up, doing four, then five, then six hits in quick succession.

The dummies were made of hard plastic. After the first few blows my whole hand was tingling, but as I got faster, I found my hand hurt much less.

Meanwhile poor Freddie had already scraped the skin off his knuckles and Åse was having problems because she's so small. If she wanted to hit her dummy on the head or neck she had to make a huge flying leap into the air.

As for Lars – well, he did nothing. He just stood watching us with a faraway look in his eyes. Sneydy turned to him and glared.

"Where are you, lad? Cloud cuckoo land?" he shouted.

Lars stared at the far wall.

"Cat got your tongue?"

Lars didn't reply.

Sneydy came up very close to Lars's ear. I don't know what he said, but Lars jerked to attention. Then, with his head slightly on one side, he looked at the dummy. At the back of the barn lay a German helmet. Lars walked over to the helmet, picked it up, returned and placed it on his dummy. Then he took three steps backwards.

I barely saw what happened next, but suddenly Lars charged forward and landed a ferocious blow on the dummy's chin. There was a loud crack as the dummy jerked backwards on its wire hanger and the neck joint broke apart. The German helmet clattered across the barn floor and so, too, did the dummy's head.

We all stopped
what we were
doing.

Lars, his head
bowed, returned
to where he'd been
standing. Sneydy
looked at the headless
dummy and clicked his
tongue approvingly.

"We're now going to move
on to pair work," he said, as if
nothing had happened. "Remember,
all the moves are to be performed fast
and with certainty. But please be careful. This is a
practice session. Understood? No Brownie points if
you kill your sparring partner or hospitalize him."

"Or her," added Åse in a semi-whisper.

"Button your lip, Miss Jeffries!" shouted Sneydy
– and he was really bellowing now. "Do you
understand?"

"Yes, sir!" chorused everybody except Lars.

"Understood, Petersen?"

Lars didn't react.

"Petersen!"

Lars looked up slowly and nodded.

Jakob P. Stromsheim

I'm in the kitchen – Mrs Collins has just served us a sneaky elevenses of custard tarts – but I'll continue with what happened last night.

I was completely worn out by the combat lesson, but we still had orienteering to do, followed by drill. And after that the Colonel decided to cram in some shooting practice.

For supper Mrs Collins made a huge fish pie, with blackcurrant crumble for pudding. It was *so* delicious that I had thirds and afterwards I could barely prise myself out of my chair. Eventually I lumbered upstairs and I had just enough energy to fold up my clothes before I crept into my freezing cold bed. Then I found I was too tired to sleep.

My mind was racing. I thought about Mother, wondering if she was eating properly. She's had no appetite since Father went missing. And I never hear her laugh. I think she misses Father so much that she's not really living any more, just mimicking the motions. I'm sure she only keeps going for my sake.

Since I wasn't going to start snoozing any time soon, I decided to write her a letter. I switched on the reading light and was rummaging in my drawer for some notepaper, when I had a strange feeling that I was being watched.

I turned round. In the bed next to me, Lars was lying slumped over the edge of the mattress, one hand trailing on the floor. His head was on one side and his eyes were staring straight at me.

I waved a hand, but Lars didn't blink. His expression was glassy. His body was completely still and his face very pale.

He looked like he was dead.

"Lars!" I called out.

There was no reply.

Dear God! I got up and ran round to his bed. I grabbed him by the arm and shook him hard. His head jolted backwards and his body tensed up. He looked at me with utter horror, then he screamed. He screamed *very loudly*.

Freddie sat up in bed and rubbed his eyes and then, just as suddenly, Lars stopped screaming. He looked at me as if I was a madman.

"I'm sorry," I said. "I thought you were ill. Is something the matter?"

Lars shook his head. Then he put his hands over his face and sat crouched over, very, very still.

When he finally lifted his head from his hands

he spoke quietly and in Norwegian. "Sorry," he said. "I was dreaming. I thought you were someone else."

"Lars, do you always sleep with your eyes open?"

But Lars didn't reply. He just turned his head to the wall.

Åse Jeffries

1st DECEMBER 1942, DRUMINCRAIG HOUSE

Day three of Druminhell House and I've finally worked out survival tips for life here:

1. Avoid eye contact with the Colonel. Look at him and he remembers you are there and will "volunteer" you for some extra task.

2. Avoid anything whatsoever to do with Sergeant Chop-chop-chop.

3. Make friends with Mrs Collins. She has limitless supplies of sugar and cocoa powder.

I've also discovered what's in my bedroom cupboard!

It all started this afternoon. After lunch we were told to go to the library, where Mrs Collins had lit a fire. Here Colonel Armstrong introduced us to a bandy-legged little man called Albert, who was pink and slightly bent and looked just like a shrimp.

We sat down and the Colonel told us the shrimp

had a very special lesson to teach us.

The man then unrolled a soft canvas case about as long as my hand. Inside was a set of fine metal pincers and funny elongated hooks and probes which he laid out on the table.

He was here to show us how to pick a lock (the shrimp has, apparently, "done more 'ouses than we've 'ad 'ot breakfasts"). And like so many of the things we've learned here, lock picking sounds incredibly exciting but the reality is a bit more humdrum and you need to put in hours of practice and hard slog.

The shrimp got going pretty quickly. First he showed us some pictures of the inside of a standard deadbolt lock. The mechanism is made up of a series of pins that move up and down, rather like piano keys. If you want to pick a lock you have to wiggle and waggle your pick into the keyhole, find each of these pins (normally there are five), nudge them into the right position and then swivel the whole lock round.

Bingo! The lock opens.

We all had a go. I'm usually good at fiddly things,

but this was darned hard. You have to concentrate all the while and visualize the inside of the lock as you wiggle away. One false move and all the pins come crashing down and you have to start again. I found it helped if I shut my eyes and kind of let my fingers think for me. After the second or third go I began to get the hang of it. The shrimp even said I had a good set of fingers on me and wondered if I might "help him out on a job" one day. The Colonel didn't think that was at all funny.

"Don't get above yourself, Albert," he snapped.

Anyway, the shrimp seemed to have taken a shine to me, so I asked him – quietly, so the Colonel wouldn't hear – if I could keep my lock pick so I could practise. He gave me a quick nod and I hid the pick up my sleeve.

The minute the lesson was over I went straight upstairs to my bedroom to get into that creepy cupboard. The lock was a bit rusty but, after a couple of tries, I was in. The stink of mothballs would have felled a rhino, but I breathed through my mouth and plunged in. I found three fur coats in dust covers and four large cardboard boxes marked FRAGILE, but there were no nests or droppings or other signs of the mysterious scrabbling beasts.

Well, at this point, I just had to open one of the boxes, didn't I? I lifted the cardboard flaps up and…

Yeuch! Yeuch! Yeuch!

I took a great gasp of horrible mothball air.

The box was filled with rows of DEAD RATS!

They were laid out really neatly – like apples in the grocers – with cardboard under each layer. Each little rat was carefully wrapped in tissue paper with its tail sticking out of one end and its snout out of the other.

I opened the next box. More rats. And the next box. Even more rats. And the next box…

Then I did some sums. The first box I opened had twelve rats on each layer and (though I didn't delve too far) I think there were five layers.

12 rats x 5 layers = 60 rats in a box.

60 rats x 4 boxes = 240 rats.

That is A LOT OF DEAD RATS!

I unwrapped one of the rats and had a look at it. It felt kind of hard in the middle, but maybe that was rigor mortis – when the body goes hard after death. The horrible bald, pink tail was still as floppy as a worm though.

I turned the rat over and saw there were neat little stitches all along the underbelly. Jeez! The rat had been stuffed.

Is this the Colonel's hobby? After we've gone to bed does he sit up with Sergeant Sneyd lovingly stitching up dead rats? I wouldn't put it past them.

And why stuff the rats? Do the mad English have special dead rat shops? I wouldn't put that past them either...

I'm in bed now and I've put all the boxes back in the creepy cupboard. This discovery hasn't dealt with the mystery scratching sounds, but I realize the noise must come from behind the cupboard. It's probably rats in the wainscot. Maybe they're relatives of the dead rats in the boxes and have come to pay their last respects.

Åse Jeffries

2ND DECEMBER 1942, DRUMINCRAIG HOUSE

This morning there was more of that weird horizontal rain. I know Scotland is meant to be beautiful and all that, but it's so darned miserable. They wouldn't know the sun here if it bit them in the backside. (You may wonder why somebody who is half-Norwegian is complaining about a bit of cold, but Norway's different – there it's a bright, sparkly, magical kind of cold.)

Anyway, as always happens when the weather becomes unspeakable, the Colonel pointed his long nose in the air and rubbed his hands together and announced it was time for a "wee stroll".

We were outside for four hours. FOUR HOURS! We marched in single file along a mountain ridge with a twenty-metre drop on one side. I was just behind the new boy, Lars. He's a real Mr No-Smiles-No-Chat. He walks quicker than a mountain goat and clearly has leg muscles of braided titanium – he never *ever* stops for a breather. But I wasn't going to be outdone by a boy, so I ended up almost running to keep up.

When we got back, Mrs Collins was standing at the front door.

"Drop scones for the children in the library," she said, giving the Colonel a thunderous look.

There was a huge fire in the library, and a tray piled with scones and fruit cake. We ate and ate and ate – even Fred got to the point where he'd had enough. And afterwards, while we were slouching around in the armchairs, I told Jakob about the rats.

He didn't believe me. So just to prove it to him, I went to my bedroom, got the lock pick out of my toilet bag (where I've been hiding it), unlocked the cupboard, took out a rat and brought it downstairs. Then I crept up behind Jakob's armchair and dangled the rat under his nose.

He laughed, reached up and grabbed it. Then he

threw the rat to Fred, who gave a little yelp of surprise and flung it straight into the fire.

A second later:

WHUMPH!

An almighty explosion shook the room. Red-hot embers flew in all directions, window panes cracked, books came crashing down off the shelves and evil black smoke poured out of the fireplace. There was a horrible smell of burnt hair.

The library now looked like this:

Fireplace: entirely black.

Carpet: entirely covered in ash.

Armchairs: entirely covered in ash.

Fred: also covered in ash, spectacles wonky and blackened, no eyebrows.

Then the Colonel came in. He seemed curious, rather than angry. He certainly didn't look shocked or surprised – maybe people blow themselves up all the time at Drumincraig.

"Well, well, well," he said quietly. "What happened?"

"Err … sorry, ummh, we – ahem – threw something in the fire," I stumbled.

"My dear Miss Jeffries, *what* precisely did you throw in the fire?"

"Err," I replied in a little rodent-sized voice, "a rat."

"Ah," said the Colonel in a well-that-explains-everything tone of voice. "Was it, by any chance, a stuffed rat from your bedroom cupboard?"

"Yes, sir," I said in a teensy, weensy mouse-voice.

"Hmm…" The Colonel rubbed his chin thoughtfully. "From the *locked* bedroom cupboard that you were told to leave well alone."

"Yes, sir." My voice was positively gnat-sized now.

Colonel Armstrong gave me one of his beady looks. "You do realize, Miss Jeffries, that the rat had twenty-five grams of plastic explosive in its belly?"

"Oh, crikey!" I said. I've done enough explosives training to know that twenty-five grams is a good-sized charge. These rats weren't just fun and games fireworks.

There was a slightly awkward pause, and then Jakob asked what we had all been wondering.

"Sir? *Why* was the dead rat stuffed with explosives?"

"Och, I suppose there's no harm you knowing now," said the Colonel. He spoke in a slightly dreamy voice. "It was a nice wee sabotage project we'd been

57

working on. We were planning to export the rats to France. Get our people to plant 'em down in the boiler rooms of the German munitions factories and transport depots. The idea was that if a boilerman found one of these rats he'd just pick it up with his shovel and fling it in the fire. You know, a fire's the best place for them. Nobody likes a dead rat in their wastepaper bin…"

"Or in their bedroom cupboard," I murmured, but the Colonel's face didn't flicker.

"Sadly, it didn't work," he continued. "Somehow German intelligence found out about the idea and factory workers have been warned to look out for stuffed rats. Cat got out of the bag, as it were. So now we're left with hundreds of stuffed rats. Terrible waste. Don't know how to shift them." He gave us one of his wry grins. "A bit disappointing, don't you think? I'd have hoped for a bigger bang than that."

Then he wandered out, saying he needed to look for Mrs Collins. Meanwhile Fred came over to the tea tray, blew the ash off a slice of fruit cake and stuffed it in his mouth.

Tonight, when I came upstairs and opened my toilet bag, I found my lock pick was still there. But wrapped around it was a small note in the Colonel's copperplate hand. It said:

Jakob P. Stromsheim

6TH DECEMBER 1942, DRUMINCRAIG HOUSE

I'm afraid I've let the log slip. The first day Åse gave it back to me I was too tired to write anything. Then another day went by, and another and another.

Four days have passed and such a lot has happened that I don't think I'm quite the same person I was when I first came. I can now assemble and fire a Sten gun in 36 seconds (48 seconds with a blindfold). And I'm becoming pretty fluent at Morse, although I'm not as good as Freddie – I bet he even thinks in dashes and dots.

Freddie's eyebrows have started to grow in again. And Lars has settled in as much as he ever will – he's a loner and never talks when he doesn't have to.

He does have one strange quirk, though – a fear of being crammed into small spaces. He has twice refused to go on Sneydy's potholing expeditions and I was rather surprised when the Colonel let him off.

The basic training in Monmouthshire got us fit and able to fire rifles and do parachute jumps. But this "fine-tuning" (as the Colonel calls it) has been harder than I could ever have believed. I've climbed more cliffs and wobbled along more tightropes than I can count. We memorize routes, we always travel as if in enemy territory, keeping to the trees and away from the skyline. We're also doing a lot of skiing, but it's not like skiing in Norway. Here it's all howling winds and black ice.

All this, as Colonel Armstrong likes to say, is very "character building". So too are the classes on how to stand up to enemy interrogation, or jump from a fast-moving train, or kill a mad dog with your bare hands (I'm not going to write about that – it's too gruesome).

We've also discovered that the Colonel and Sergeant Sneyd have a particular love of blades. They've given each of us our own specially weighted, extra-sharp, double-bladed combat knife – a Fairbairn-Sykes fighting knife. The sergeant insists that we each have to be able to wield our knife "as delicately as an artist uses a paintbrush". And, like artists, we have to act instinctively – the moves must be quick as reflexes. So we practise and we practise and we practise.

Today we finally found out what our mission is to be (I hope I've got Freddie's explanations correct – I only understand the science very hazily).

It started with a special meeting that the Colonel called this morning.

SOE | SPECIAL OPERATIONS EXECUTIVE

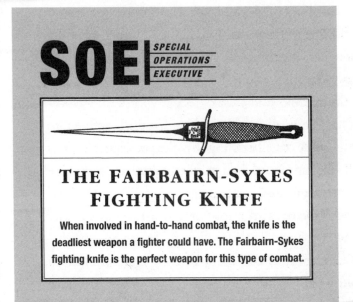

THE FAIRBAIRN-SYKES FIGHTING KNIFE

When involved in hand-to-hand combat, the knife is the deadliest weapon a fighter could have. The Fairbairn-Sykes fighting knife is the perfect weapon for this type of combat.

THE FAIRBAIRN-SYKES FIGHTING KNIFE

CARRYING THE KNIFE
Make sure that the knife's sheath is securely attached to your clothing so that you can draw the knife quickly. Constant daily practise is needed to ensure you can draw the knife quickly. Concealing the knife may also be desireable if you need to surprise your opponent.

Good balance – the blade is perfectly weighted so that the hilt sits well back in the palm and won't be dragged from the hand, even when the knife is being held in a loose grip.

Hilt fits eaily and comfortably in the hand. Grip roughened for maximum purchase in wet weather.

Sharp stabbing point.

Sharp cutting edges – essential for severing arteries cleanly. Arteries which are torn by a blunt knife have a tendancy to contract and therefore stop bleeding, potentially allowing your opponent to continue to fight.

KEY FEATURES

It was about 10.30 a.m. when we were summoned to the library. There we found the Colonel standing in front of the fireplace with his arms behind his back. Something about his manner told me he had something important to say.

When we'd all sat down the Colonel nodded to Sneydy, who was hovering by the window. Sneydy closed the curtains and, as they're green, a strange aquarium-like light immediately filled the room. The Colonel looked down at us from over his glasses (why can't he ever just take them off?) and began his speech.

"We've come to the time when you children need to be told what's in store for you. As you know, we have chosen you to go on an important mission. It won't be easy and it won't be safe. Indeed, I cannot even assure you that you'll survive. But you'll be risking your necks for a cause more important than anything you can possibly imagine. This mission may decide the course of the war. And if it doesn't go ahead the whole of London – eight million people – could be destroyed in a flash."

The Colonel paused for a moment to let this awful idea sink in, then he went on. "First of all I need to give you a wee demonstration."

He took a glass of water from the coffee table and held it up in the air.

"You see this water? Anything unusual about it?"

I stared blankly at the glass. It seemed perfectly ordinary. I looked over at Freddie and he shrugged – he clearly didn't think there was anything unusual either.

The Colonel unscrewed the lid of an ice box and, with a pair of tongs, he picked out two ice cubes and plopped them into the glass of water.

He held up the glass again.

"Anything unusual now?"

There was something strange about it, but I just couldn't put my finger on it.

"Nothing unusual?" the Colonel asked me again. He was getting a little impatient. "Have a closer look. Take a sip if you want."

The Colonel passed the glass to me and I took a sip. It was perfectly ordinary water. But there was something not quite right. What was it? Then, at last, I twigged.

"The ice! Ice is meant to float. This ice has sunk!"

The Colonel rolled his eyes. "Well, that took you a while! Does anyone know what this is? Miss Jeffries? Petersen? Haukerd?"

"It's not ordinary ice,"

said Freddie, twiddling with a bit of fluff on his jumper and staring up at a little brownish watercolour on the wall. He continued, "It must be heavy water – deuterium oxide, or ^2H_2O. It's similar to water – H_2O – but the hydrogen atom is made of the heavy isotope deuterium. There's a proton and a neutron in the nucleus of each atom, instead of just one proton on its own as you get in an ordinary hydrogen atom." And he did a little diagram for us.

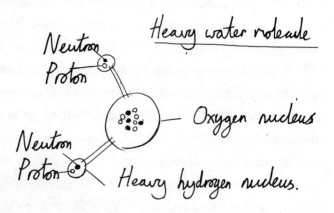

"This kind of ice takes longer to melt – its melting point is 3.8 degrees Celsius. Heavy water is a very stable medium for chemical reactions. There are some really interesting things that you can do with it. Am I boring you all to death?"

"Go on," said the Colonel.

"Heavy water is used as a moderator – it can help slow down and control chemical reactions. A few years ago there was a lot of work done with splitting the atom. It's a new field called nuclear science. Take uranium, for example. It's the heaviest element and it's fissile – in other words it has a big atom that can be broken apart. If you bombard uranium with neutrons and split it, an enormous quantity of heat is produced. But what's even more important is this: when a uranium atom splits you also get other neutrons coming away at the side of the atom. It's a bit like when you chop a loaf of bread and crumbs fall down. Well, these neutrons – the atomic crumbs, if you like – then collide with other atoms, leading to more atoms splitting. You get a chain reaction that increases exponentially. One atom splits, then two atoms, then four atoms, then eight atoms, then sixteen and so on. You can generate enormous amounts of heat and that means you can cause huge explosions – far greater than anything we've seen before."

"How d'you know all this?" asked the Colonel. For once he looked a bit discombobulated.

"It's amazing what you can order through Barnet public library," replied Freddie, fingers still twiddling on that bit of fluff. Then he added, "Well, you *used* to be able to do that. There's been nothing published recently. Must be to do with the war—"

Freddie stopped. He blinked slowly. "Excuse me, sir. But if scientists can control chain reactions, they could make huge, super-powerful bombs. Is this what you meant when you were talking earlier about London being destroyed?"

The Colonel smiled. "Haukerd, you may have two left feet and be the worst shot this side of the Great Glen, but you've got a good brain in there. And you've hit the nail on the head. We know that German physicists are working on making a bomb – a bomb which will harness the energy from splitting the uranium atom. This bomb will be a hundred times more powerful than anything we've ever seen. And if Adolf Hitler gets his hands on such a bomb, he'll be able to obliterate London, Washington, New York. You name it. There's just one thing he lacks…" Here the Colonel raised the glass of water, and jiggled the ice cubes.

"Heavy water," said Freddie tonelessly.

The Colonel looked at the glass in his hand. "It doesn't seem like much, but this stuff is pricey. It's difficult and time-consuming to produce – there is a complex extraction process. And at present the only place in the world that makes significant quantities of heavy water is a hydro-electric plant in Vemork, up in the mountains of Norway."

The Colonel gave us one of his grim smiles. "And that's where you lot come in. Your mission is to go into occupied Norway. We will parachute you into the mountains of the Hardanger Plateau, west of Oslo. From there you will make your way to the Norsk Hydro power station at Vemork. The Norsk Hydro is perched on the edge of a cliff, hence all the climbing practice you've been doing. You'll enter the basement of the building, lay charges and then escape. So how does that sound?"

I just sat there numbly in my chair. Nobody said anything. I remembered that in one of the Colonel's letters at the beginning of the log he suggested we might "come to grief" on the trip, so I simply didn't know what to think.

I looked at Åse, who was looking at me with an expression that was part smile and part grimace.

"Does anyone feel they don't want to go ahead with this?" the Colonel continued. "Does anyone want to leave the room? There's no obligation to take part, though you know what your king and your country expect of you."

"How do we get away afterwards?" asked Åse.

"You'll make your way to Sweden, which is about

400 kilometres away. You'll have skis, of course, and some of it's a nice downhill run. When you get to Sweden, one of our operatives will take care of you."

The Colonel looked at each of us – first Lars, then Åse, then Freddie. They all nodded.

Lastly the Colonel turned to me.

His words were still ringing in my ears. Could I, Jakob Stromsheim, really alter the course of the war? Maybe I'd die. Maybe my whole life had been building up to this moment. Was this what I was destined to do? And what about Mother? What would she think? That was what clinched it for me – thinking what Mother would want me to do.

So, fool that I am, I nodded too.

The Colonel gave a quick smile and said to Sergeant Sneyd, "I thought we'd picked the right chaps for the job."

"I'm not a chap," hissed Åse.

The Colonel raised an eyebrow and smiled. "Chaps and *chappess*," he corrected himself. "There are two things I want you to realize. First, you've all been picked for different reasons; each of you has a specific purpose in this mission. Haukerd, you are in charge of communications. Miss Jeffries, your prime duty is explosives, but we are also relying on your size to enable you to squeeze into tiny spaces. Petersen, you are the outdoor survival expert. And Stromsheim, you must lead the mission. Each of you has to do your particular bit and more. Each of you is responsible. There's no room for passengers.

"My second point is this. Stromsheim has the temperament and the judgement and the steadiness of character that are perhaps the most important of human qualities, and his job is to hold the party together. As for the rest of you, what Stromsheim says goes. He is the leader. He decides. You do what he says, even if you don't agree with him."

"But sir," I said, blushing slightly. "Why don't you just bomb the hydro plant from the sky? Surely that would be easier?"

"You're quite right – that would be far simpler," replied the Colonel. "But it's risky. As Petersen knows, there are people living in that valley – at least 2,000 in the village of Rjukan. If we accidentally hit the Mosvatn dam, billions of litres of water would sweep down the valley, obliterating everyone and everything for miles around. There are also some liquid ammonia storage tanks at the bottom of the valley. If you've ever seen an ammonia explosion you wouldn't wish that on your worst enemy. So I'm afraid sabotage is the only answer."

"How long do we have to prepare for this?" I asked.

"You leave on the next full moon. That's two days from now," said the Colonel.

"But, sir, it's December!" I blurted out. "We're landing on the Hardanger Plateau. It'll be snow-bound. And what about the blizzards? You can die in minutes up there."

"The temperature goes down to minus thirty degrees Celsius," added Freddie.

The Colonel, who was reaching into his pocket for a scrap of paper as we spoke, nodded. "You're quite right, lad. And the wind-chill factor can make it twice as cold."

"Isn't this madness?" I asked. "Even wild animals starve to death up there. Nobody goes up on the Hardanger in winter."

"Precisely," said the Colonel. "Nobody goes there. So nobody will see you. You couldn't have a better hiding place."

"Hold it, everyone!" Åse was on her feet. "Why are *we* going? Colonel, why do you want kids for this mission? Why aren't you using trained paratroopers? They're bigger. They're stronger. Why *us*?"

"As you know, we've already lost a whole team of special agents, so we're trying a different approach. Now have a look at this," the Colonel continued nonchalantly, "and this concerns you in particular,

Miss Jeffries." The Colonel's piece of paper was now flat on the coffee table. It showed a diagram of the side elevation of a complex, six-storey building.

"This is the Vemork power plant. And here next to the door—" the Colonel's finger rested on the side of the tower where the steps ran down into the basement of the plant "—is an electrical cable duct about thirty centimetres square. It's the one unguarded way down to the heavy water stores. No adult could fit through this passageway. But you, Miss Jeffries, could scuttle down it fast as a ferret. Though you'd better not eat too many of Mrs Collins' puddings or you might just get stuck." He saw the expression on Åse's face and added quickly, "I'm joking, of course.

"And there's another reason for sending you to Norway. There is the element of surprise. Nobody suspects children. Nobody thinks a bunch of kids could bomb a power station. They think children wouldn't have the strength or stamina. They're right to an extent. The most important thing will be to eat enough to maintain your strength.

"And of course, if anything goes wrong and you are picked up, you must stay silent. Don't try to be clever under interrogation. Don't try and explain. Say nothing. The Germans aren't very kind to saboteurs. And they know what we're after."

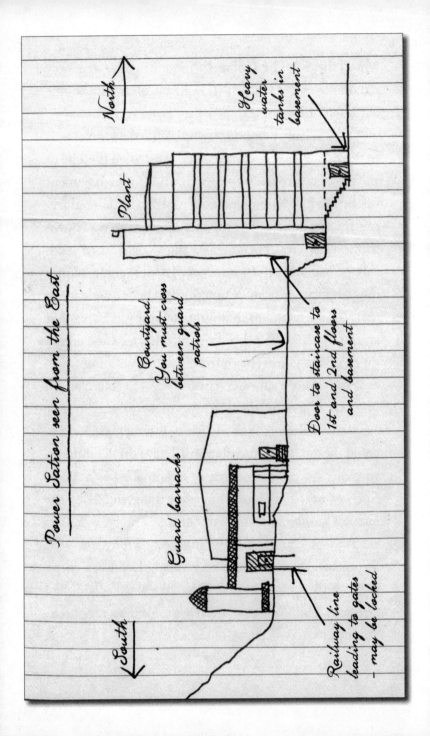

Jakob P. Stromsheim

I'm writing this in bed.

For lunch Mrs Collins surpassed herself: there was fillet steak with mountains of chips, followed by caramel apple turnovers. Yet the meal was a sombre affair. We just sat there, lost in thought. No one spoke and no one had much appetite. Even Freddie didn't finish what was on his plate.

All through the meal something was nagging at the back of my brain. Immediately after lunch, I went up the winding stairs to the Colonel's study and knocked on the door.

"Enter," he growled.

The Colonel was sitting back with his feet on his desk and his pipe in his mouth. The air was thick with smoke and the Colonel cut it with a curved dagger that he flicked from hand to hand – *swish, swish, swish*. Every now and then he spun the knife in a high arc through the air and caught it by the hilt.

I must have been gawping stupidly at him, for suddenly the Colonel spoke quite sharply.

"Well, what is it, boy?" *Swish, swish, swish*, went the dagger.

"Well, sir…" I began, trying not to look at the knife.

"Spit it out!"

Swish, swish, swish.

I didn't know how to start the conversation, so I began with a question.

"Sir," I stumbled, "what are the chances that any of us will return from this mission?"

He considered this for a moment and then said, "You're children and you're facing impossible odds. The chances were never going to be good."

"You say 'impossible odds'. Do you really think our chances are that bad?"

"Och, technically speaking, you're bound to get killed," said the Colonel amiably. He chewed on his pipe for a minute and then added, "As I said, you're children. Nobody in their right mind sends children on such a mission. But personally I see things differently. I think people always underestimate kids. I know what you can do. The assault courses you and the others have been on at Drumincraig are no different from those tackled by our adult trainees. Maybe a few more hand-holds on the climbs, but that's the only real difference."

Listening to the Colonel talk about the prospect of being "technically" dead seemed to focus my mind. I had to tell him what had been worrying me.

"Sir, I do have one real concern about this mission.

It's my mother. Ever since my father went missing things have been a bit difficult for her. I know that you want me to go, and I know that she would want me to go. I would be letting both of you down if I didn't. But I don't think I can leave her. She needs me at home."

The Colonel put his knife down. "Jakob, don't worry," he said quietly. "We sent one of our men to visit your mother on Tuesday – we needed parental permission before we asked any of you to do this."

"And what did she say?" I asked.

"She said that your father would have been proud of you."

Would have been?

That *would have been* felt like a kick in the guts. Father is not dead. He's missing in action. He could be a prisoner of war. He could be lying low behind enemy lines. Or he could be out on some operation with a faulty radio transmitter. Anything.

Nobody – until now – has ever said that my father is dead. Does "missing" really mean "dead"? Has everyone else quietly buried him in their minds? Is it only me that holds out any hope?

To my surprise – for he never touches anyone – the Colonel leaned over and put a hand on my shoulder. "I'm sorry, sonny. War brings grief and hardship to us all, but it also brings out qualities that we never knew we had. In the days to come your loss will become your strength. We often find the best agents are those with the least to lose."

After I left the Colonel's office I went for a walk in the grounds. The rest of the evening has passed me by in a blur. I only hope that tomorrow there'll be something to distract me from my thoughts.

Jakob P. Stromsheim

7TH DECEMBER 1942

I'm writing this sitting on a pile of logs after the worst night of my life. I really can't believe I'm still alive.

It all started last night.

I woke suddenly in the dead of night. It was a horrible feeling. I opened my eyes. Two large men in overcoats – I couldn't see their faces in the darkness – were by my bed. One of them was tying a gag round my mouth, the other was binding my feet.

This is a nightmare, I thought. *I'm only dreaming this.*

But, of course, I wasn't.

I tried to cry out, but there was something clogging my mouth and blocking off my tongue. A voice with a heavy accent hissed, "Quiet".

I tried to wriggle free, but one of the men swore in German and wrenched the gag so tight that it cut into the corners of my mouth. The other man at the foot of the bed pulled my legs down hard.

So I had to lie there, trussed up from head to toe – hands and feet and knees all bound together. I could move my neck and there was just enough light for me to see that Lars's bed was empty, with the bedclothes all jumbled on the floor. Did he get away, I wondered, or had they got him too? What about Freddie?

One man grabbed my shoulders and a cloth bag was thrust down over my head. Now I could see nothing at all – just blackness – a stuffy, hot, airless blackness. Then I was picked up by the waist and roughly hoisted over one of the men's shoulders, like a sack of coal.

The man set off, walking quickly along the corridor and upper landing and down the stone staircase. With every step he took, my head bumped against his back.

I stopped trying to struggle. There was no point when I was so tightly bound and I certainly didn't want to be accidentally dropped head first on the stone stairs. Anyway, I'd got my mind on more important things – like breathing. The hood was made of some heavy, closely woven material and I had to fight for air – taking deep breaths in through my nose, though nothing seemed to be getting to my lungs. I felt sick and dizzy. How long would it be before I blacked out?

At the foot of the stairs the man turned into the

corridor that led past the boiler room to the kitchen. The back door opened and I felt the cold air as we came out onto the gravel. The man crossed the back yard. A second later, he bent down, gave a heave and a grunt and I was tossed into the air.

In the blackness, I tried to put out my hands to break my fall – but they were bound tight. I landed on my side, smashing my forehead against a sharp corner. I cried out, but only a feeble muffled squeak got through the gag.

I was lying on a damp metal floor, the cold seeping through my pyjamas. The wound on my head thudded and I could feel warm liquid running down my face. I curled up to try and keep warm. I remembered that earlier in the night I had wanted some distraction – now I had it in spades.

A minute later, a door slammed and an engine started up. Suddenly the floor under me began to move. I was in the back of a lorry or a Landrover. The driver accelerated fast – he crashed along the bumpy old driveway at bone-breaking speed. And of course I couldn't hold on to anything to steady myself, so I just bumped painfully up and down like a loose ball bearing.

The driver turned on to the tarmac road. Here he went even faster, screeching round the corners, sending me sliding helplessly from side to side, banging into the seats. The road wound on endlessly. I was freezing cold and hardly able to breathe, and I was still being buffeted back and forth, back and forth. I soon lost any sense of time.

Eventually the vehicle stopped and the back door opened.

"Out! Get out!" yelled the voice with the heavy, Germanic accent. Someone grabbed me by the arms and pulled me on to the ground.

I was standing on wet cement or tarmac – I knew that, for I was in bare feet. And I could hear a large engine running nearby.

Someone undid the rope tying my feet together.

"Move! Walk!"

I couldn't see where I was, so I took a small, careful step forward.

"Faster!" yelled the man.

Something small and hard and round prodded me in the small of the back. I stumbled, but a hand grabbed my arm to stop me falling and marched me along.

"Steps," said the voice.

We mounted a short flight of metal steps that clanked and swayed like a ladder. Through my hood I could smell diesel fumes and I realized I must be climbing into an aircraft.

Once we were inside, the man shouted, "Down!"

I knelt down.

"Down!"

A sharp kick in the side, just below the ribcage, toppled me onto my side. Quickly I curled into a foetal position and put my hands up to cover my face. I waited for the next blow, but nobody hit me again. I felt the engine purr into gear. Hurried voices were speaking in German.

The plane juddered down the runway and I felt a peculiar floaty sensation of release as the plane lifted upwards into the sky. I was too tired now to feel frightened and too tired to feel self-pitying. I was also too cold to sleep. I had no idea what would happen next – I could be going anywhere. But I knew that whatever lay ahead, it was going to be worse than what had just happened. I would need all my strength.

Time passed. My legs were still unbound and every so often I tried turning over, believing that in another position I wouldn't be quite so uncomfortable. I tried to move as quietly as possible – the last thing I wanted was another kick in the ribs – but the position I ended up in was always worse than before.

After one of these moves, I heard boots walking towards me. I huddled up tight waiting for the blow, but instead someone grabbed my arm and pulled up my pyjama sleeve. Then something cold was rubbed on to a patch of my upper arm. I smelled the disinfectant – it must have been a swab of cotton wool. That was strange – first they hit you and half suffocated you, then they treated you with cotton wool.

I felt the needle go in, and with it came a rising wave of heaviness. Then there was nothing.

I woke to find the wound on my forehead throbbing. The strange heaviness was still there and it felt as if I'd been unconscious for a long time – maybe hours, maybe days.

Where was I? I wasn't in the aircraft any longer. I wasn't on the move. There was straw underneath me.

I came to the conclusion I must be somewhere behind enemy lines. Maybe in Germany. Or Belgium. Maybe the Netherlands. Wherever it was, someone had cared for me, even if it was in a rough and ready manner. There was something heavy over me that smelled of mud and sweat and old tobacco – a greatcoat, probably. They'd taken the hood off my head as well, so I was just blindfolded. And some light was penetrating the blindfold, so it was daytime, wherever I was.

And, thank goodness, I no longer had the gag. I could breathe easily. But my mouth felt very dry, and I was thirsty. I wanted water. A long, cool glass of water. As long as they gave me water, I'd be all right.

More time passed. I had cramp in my right leg and I shifted around groggily under the smelly greatcoat or sacking or whatever it was that was covering me. My thoughts returned to Drumincraig. I thought of my mother. I thought of water. I thought of orange juice, of soda water, of pineapple juice, of the lemonade Mother used to make with little bits of lemon peel floating on the top. But mostly I thought about water. Cool water. Lots of it.

I heard a key rattle in a lock – a big clunky door was being opened only a metre or so away.

"Get up!" It was the same thick German voice.

I tried to get up, but with my hands bound together and the cramp in my right leg and the greatcoat in the way, I moved slowly.

The man snorted, grabbed me by the arm and hoisted me to my feet. My knees felt weak and wobbly.

"Walk!" shouted the man. And, again, there was something small and hard and round jabbing into the small of my back. I realized now it was a gun.

I walked forward. After a few yards the man thrust me through a doorway to the left. The door slammed behind me.

A man's voice said something in German. Someone cut the ropes round my wrist and then my blindfold was removed. The light was blinding. I blinked pathetically and after a few moments I could see my new surroundings.

I was in a small white room with a mirrored panel along one wall. Behind a table sat two men. One man, fit and thickset, was wearing a German army officer's uniform with a leather greatcoat and knee-high boots. His hair was short and almost white-blond, his eyes blue and very hard. His companion looked older; grey and balding with half-moon glasses. He was dressed in an old-fashioned faded suit and in front of him lay a sheaf of papers. His face was lined and tired.

The army officer spoke first.

"Name?"

"Jakob. Jakob Stromsheim."

"SIR!" bellowed the officer.

"Sir," I repeated.

The officer looked me up and down with some distaste.

"Stromsheim, where are the shoes?"

"I haven't got any." Then, quickly, I added, "sir."

"Your feet are dirty! You cannot stand here with feet like that! Clean them!"

The officer was quite right – my feet were black with dirt. But what was I to do? I bent down and started to wipe my toes with the cuff of my pyjama top.

"Stop!" he yelled.

"Yes, sir," I said.

"Fool!" he shouted. "That way your clothes become dirty!"

I just looked at him. What on earth was I to do?

"Lick!" shouted the officer.

I sat down cross-legged on the floor. My feet stank of engine oil and I was sure I was going to be sick. But I just got down to it – I shut my eyes and slowly started licking, trying all the time not to think about what I was doing. Between each lick I wanted to spit the dirt out of my mouth, but if I so much as paused the man started shouting at me again. So I just kept on licking – licking and swallowing, licking and swallowing and trying not to wretch.

After what seemed like an eternity, I heard a chair scrape backwards. The army officer walked round to my side of the table, pulled me to my feet and then gave me a kick in the backside that sent me skidding across the floor. My head smashed against the brick wall. For a minute the world seemed to swirl around. And I wondered if I'd cracked my skull, because I was seeing stars. I slowly slithered down the wall on to the concrete. I needed water. Cold, clear water.

"Lift him up," said a weary voice that must have belonged to the older man.

The officer hauled me up and threw me into a chair. Then he turned on a very bright lamp and shone it directly into my face.

I tried to turn away, but the officer grabbed my hair and jerked my head back towards the light.

"What were you doing in that house, Stromsheim?" he asked.

"On holiday, sir," I said. Even if I shut my eyes the light still bored into my eyeballs.

"You were going somewhere, were you not?"

"No, sir."

The officer yanked at my hair again.

"I said, 'You were going somewhere, were you not?'"

"Nowhere, sir." My eyes were watering. I remembered the advice in the SOE notes on interrogation. I had to act stupid. Say nothing. The prospect of pain is worse than the pain itself.

The officer brought out a long black baton from inside his greatcoat. He held it in front of my face.

"So what were you doing?" His mouth was very close to my ear.

"Adventure holiday, sir."

"What?" he hissed.

"Adventure holiday, sir."

The officer raised the baton up above my head and paused for a second. I hunched my shoulders and cringed in anticipation… The baton came crashing down and landed with a great thud on the table in front of me. It had passed millimetres from my head.

At this point the older man in the suit gestured to the officer to stop and said something in German.

Then the older man looked at me. His smile was tired, but it seemed genuine. "Now, Jakob. It's nice to meet you. Don't be frightened. Nothing will happen to you if you behave yourself. You'd be surprised how much we already know. We have much information. Your friends – they've been most helpful."

I kept my face blank. They couldn't have cracked. It wasn't true. It just wasn't true. But how would Freddie go on without food? Freddie would do almost anything for food.

The man continued. "Where were you going? Norway or Sweden?"

Even in my befuddled state I knew this question was a good sign. The others couldn't have told them anything, or they wouldn't be asking me, would they? But it was vital that my face gave nothing away. I looked at him blankly. *Be stupid. Say as little as possible.*

"I asked a question, Jakob," said the man, a little less kindly now.

"We weren't going anywhere, sir," I replied.

The man swivelled round in his chair, opened a small cabinet behind him and brought out a tray with a jug of water and a glass.

"You must be thirsty. You would like a drink?"

"Yes please, sir," I replied. Things were looking up. Maybe the interrogation wasn't going to be so bad after all.

The man poured and I watched the cool, clear water tumble into the glass. Then, slowly, the man returned to the cabinet and removed a metal ice box. He took out two ice cubes and put them in the glass. *Plop! Plop!*

He pushed the glass across the table towards me. But, just as I reached forward to take it, he moved the glass back out of reach.

Then he smiled sadly and shook his head.

"I'm sorry. I can't give you anything now. Was it Norway you said you were going to? All I need to know is that. Then you have your drink."

I stared at the glass of cool water. I wanted it so badly, and I started to consider. Surely there couldn't be any harm in saying Norway? But then I remembered the Colonel saying that once you gave away one piece of information, you would find it hard not to say more – psychologically your interrogators would have the upper hand.

So I looked at the floor and said, "We weren't going anywhere, sir."

The officer, who was still standing behind me, grabbed my hair and wrenched my head back into the light. He took my right arm and bent it round and backwards in a half-Nelson. I let out a scream of pain.

The officer tugged the arm up a little further. Then up a little further again. I clenched my teeth as the pain shot up through my shoulder and neck. The officer pulled a little tighter still. I could feel that the bones and ligaments in my arm could go no further. Soon they would snap.

I shut my eyes and counted. Five ... ten ... fifteen ... twenty. I reached sixty before the floor began to lurch. Only then did the officer release his grip.

"You can have your drink now," said the man in the suit.

He threw the water in my face.

The interrogation went on for what seemed like hours. Repeatedly the men made me stand, they made me stare at the light, they bent my arms and fingers back, they scrunched my knuckles, they kicked me round the room and threw me against the wall and, once in a while, threatened to whack me with the truncheon. The officer in uniform did most of the hitting and kicking and the tired man in the suit asked the questions. And, though plenty more glasses were poured out, they never did let me drink any water.

And, every so often, the man in the suit changed tack. His voice would soften. He offered me anything I wanted: water, lemonade, a warm bath, steak and chips, a balloon ride. (He got quite inventive at times.)

I know this sounds strange, but after a while the water became almost unimportant. As things got worse I grew more and more light-headed, as if I was watching what was happening to me from a great distance.

And somehow, I stood my ground. Repeatedly

I looked at the floor and said I didn't know anything. Again and again in my mind I counted five … ten … fifteen … twenty … and just hoped they would kill me soon. Then it would all be over.

At last the guard came and took me away. There wasn't much fight left in me by then, so nobody bothered with a blindfold or handcuffs. And I certainly wasn't up to escaping. I just stumbled along the corridor with the guard behind me. When I reached my cell I lay down on the straw, tucked the filthy old greatcoat around me and fell immediately into a deep, dreamless sleep.

Later I was roused by the sound of someone opening the heavy metal door. Light shone in from the corridor. A very tall, thin, stooped figure carried in a tray holding a jug of water and a glass.

My head pounded. My eyelids were heavy and my body ached all over.

I found myself staring at the tray thinking, *Oh no, we're going to do the glass of water game again.*

The tall stooped figure put the tray down. Alongside the jug and the glass was a small plate of custard creams.

I half closed my eyes. All I really wanted to do was sleep.

"Good afternoon, Jakob," said a voice I knew so well.

I looked up. Colonel Armstrong was crouched on

~~APO~~ INTERROGATION METHODS

~~Que~~stioning tricks

~~The follo~~wing may be used to trick the prisoner into offering up information:

~~* Lon~~g silences: these are intended to produce unsolicited remarks.

~~* Lon~~g silences in which the prisoner is discouraged from talking. The interrogator ~~may th~~en say something like, "Don't answer yet. Just think. Then tell us the truth."

~~* The~~ interrogator continually refers back to the same question, but changes his ~~appro~~ach.

~~* The~~ prisoner is shown a "confession" by a colleague.

~~* The~~ interrogator makes threats against the prisoner's family and friends.

A prisoner turns away from strong light

This image reprinted from *Get Tough* by Major W.E. Sykes, with permission from the publisher Paladin Press.

~~D~~iscomfiture of prisoner

~~The fo~~llowing techniques may be used to make ~~the p~~risoner uncomfortable and intimidated:

~~*~~ The prisoner is made to face strong light, ~~an~~d is unable to see the examiner properly.

~~*~~ The interrogation is carried out by ~~a~~ single examiner, who continues ~~in~~definitely so that the prisoner ~~be~~comes exhausted.

~~*~~ The prisoner is made to stand with ~~h~~is back to the examiner, with his ~~~~arms above his head.

* The interrogation is carried out by two examiners. The first plays the "bully" who makes the prisoner angry or frightened by using threats and throwing things. The second puts clear, concise questions. If the prisoner does not talk, he may be beaten.

* As above, but with a third interrogator who is friendly, maybe offering the prisoner food and drink. This interrogator will try to lull the prisoner into indiscretion.

3. Counter-measures

When facing interrogation, try to stick to the following guidelines:

* Speak slowly, clearly and firmly. Do not answer simple questions immediately and hesitate with the more difficult ones.

* Do not be clever or abusive. Create the impression of being an averagely stupid, honest citizen. Interrogators are not impressed by tears or heroics.

* Avoid replies that lead to further questions.

* Do not express personal affection or interest in anybody. This can be used against you later.

* Beware of the apparently foolish interrogator. This may be a trap.

* Do not be bluffed by the interrogator who pretends he has knowledge of your British connections. It is likely that, over a period of time, the Gestapo has learned some facts about the SOE.

A prisoner will be frightened when he can't see what is to happen to him the ground beside the tray, stuffing his pipe.

How on earth could the Colonel, of all people, be here in the cell with me? I must have been dreaming.

The Colonel smiled. "When you're ready, come outside and join the others. Mrs Collins is cooking up a feast."

"Come outside?" I bumbled, completely confused.

The Colonel continued. "Sorry about the rough handling. We had to test you, lad. You and the others have all done well. You're still at Drumincraig, of course. The journey in the aeroplane was just ten minutes round Inverness airport, and then we brought you straight back here."

"And the Germans?" I asked. I felt so relieved that it hadn't occurred to me (yet!) to be angry with him.

"They're out-of-work actors. Good, aren't they? And they'll work for almost nothing. So many theatres have had to close because of the war." Colonel Armstrong looked around the cell, with its bare, windowless walls and filthy straw. He gave a satisfied nod. "We're in the outhouse beyond the shooting range. I'm quite pleased with this little prison, though I say it myself. Quite convincing, don't you think?"

When I emerged from my cell I could see the back courtyard only thirty metres away – near enough for the cooking smells to reach me. I'd been so near, and yet so far away.

Freddie, Lars and Åse, all looking dirty and hollow-eyed, were sitting on a small dry-stone wall waiting for me. Åse gave me a big hug.

"I thought I'd never see you again," I said.

Åse grinned. "I've got a huge bruise that's the same shape as a map of Ireland. But Fred's is even better."

Freddie rolled up his trouser leg. He'd lost most of the skin on his left shin.

"What happened?" I asked.

"It was during the questioning. This big German chap threw me across the room and I landed on a radiator."

"Did you annoy him?"

"Not really, but I did answer all his questions in Latin. Thought it might keep him on his toes."

I looked at Åse. And, despite our wobbly knees and bruised ribs, we started to laugh.

Though we'd been gone less than a day – and we hadn't exactly been far away – coming back into the courtyard at Drumincraig felt like returning home after a long journey. Mrs Collins came out of the kitchen to greet us. She clasped us all suffocatingly in her huge bosom (Lars screwed up his eyes and winced but Mrs C paid not the blindest bit of attention and hugged him all the tighter). Then, at last, she let us go upstairs to get washed and changed for lunch.

We had the rest of the day off. And although Colonel Armstrong had promised us there would be no extra lessons, Åse quickly pointed out that if he saw us hanging around he was sure to find us something to do.

So after lunch, we gathered up blankets and pillows from our beds and crept down to the boiler room in the basement. And, while the others made a big nest of bedclothes on top of the wood pile, I sneaked two bottles of Mrs Collins' lemonade and a packet of Bourbon biscuits from the kitchen.

So that's where we are now, settled down for a lovely long afternoon of lounging and log writing and biscuit nibbling. And it's been made all the more wonderful because we all know that soon there will be no more days like this. Soon we'll be fighting for our lives. But that's in the future. Not now. Now we're just going to take things easy.

Åse can take over the log now. I bet she has some pretty bitter things to say about Colonel Armstrong.

Åse Jeffries

We are just back from the Colonel's latest lovely surprise: a day and a night in an interrogation cell with one-way mirrors on the walls so that he and Chop-chop-chop could secretly watch us being duffed over. The scary German interrogators may only have been actors – though they do seem to have "got into" their parts – but the fleas in the straw were 100 per cent genuine. I've got a little row of bites all down one arm.

We weren't put on the rack or hung upside down – that'll be for the Gestapo to do when we get caught in Norway. But it was *very* hard. I thought I was going to die. So did Jakob. Fred says he nearly gave way when they brought out a tray of little Viennese pastries and hot sausage rolls, but he pulled through by shutting his eyes and playing imaginary chess games with himself.

The only person who didn't seem shaken up was Lars. Afterwards, when we were all yacketty-yacking away, Mr No-Chat said nothing. And when Jakob asked him how he felt, Lars just shrugged and said quietly, "The real thing is far worse." He wouldn't say any more, but there was something pretty chilling in his voice and it shut everybody up.

Anyway, it's all over now. Tomorrow we leave for the air base, where we'll collect our gear and our final briefings and prepare for the Big Drop.

Area of Operations: one of the most inhospitable places on the planet.

Target: a basement only accessible via a tunnel no wider than the Colonel's pipe.

Team: Fred the Geek, Mr No-Smiles-No-Chat, Mr Sensible and eeny weeny little me.

And the up side? My chances of returning to stuck-up old Roxbury Hall are almost zero. No more dancing lessons, no more deportment classes, no more carrot pie, no more lectures on how to carry an umbrella and address the wife of a bishop. And, naturally, if it comes to a choice between instant death and elocution lessons with Mrs Forrester, I'll take instant death any day.

Åse Jeffries

Lars and I spent the whole of our last day at Drumincraig training in Sergeant Chop-chop-chop's plywood replica of the Vemork power plant basement and the heavy water containers. By the end of the day we knew the layout so well we could get in, set the charges and leave again in twenty-five minutes without ever taking our blindfolds off. Even Chop-chop-chop seems pretty pleased with our timekeeping.

When we got to the air base today, Colonel Armstrong took us to see our equipment. It was laid out in great piles along a table: tents, weapons, skis, clothes, rations... I don't know how we are going to carry it all across the Hardanger Plateau without an army of forklift trucks, or several hundred slaves. The food alone – even though it's only a four-week supply – takes up at least three rucksacks. And we're going to have to eat an awful lot of pemmican, which is a strange dried meat and fruit mixture that hardens into something a bit leathery and tastes of dog food with a lingering touch of Ribena. Bleuch!

They seem to have thought of everything, though: special woollen mitts with a separate trigger finger,

97

SOE SPECIAL OPERATIONS EXECUTIVE

Kit List: 12

Parachute Drop – Cold Weather

SKI BOOTS

LARGE SOCKS

SNOW GAITERS

WOOLLEN MITTS

WRIST-WARMERS

BALACLAVA

WIND-PROOF GLOVES

CAMOUFLAGE SUIT

RABBIT-SKIN JOCKSTRAP

BOOTS

STRING VEST

BRACES

Norwegian kroner, a little coil of waxed thread for shoe repairs, Swedish compasses, and so on. Nothing has British labels, though we do have a whole load of British army uniform for the attack itself. That has to be seen to be done by outsiders, not Norwegians, otherwise the Germans might carry out Herod-like reprisals on the local population. And the boys also have special rabbit-skin jock straps for the parachute jump – apparently they can really hurt themselves if they aren't protected.

It all looked great – if a bit scary – and then I noticed one rather important omission. Between the four of us there is only *one packet of toilet paper*.

When I pointed this out, the Colonel got very sniffy.

"You'll just have to learn to make do, Miss Jeffries. In the Middle East, the troops clean their backsides with sand. There'll be plenty of rocks and sphagnum moss…"

And then he put his left forefinger in the air – the gesture he always makes when he's going to say something very important.

"Now," he said in a hushed voice. "I have a very personal gift for each of you."

The door opened and Chop-chop-chop (for once he wasn't smiling) brought in a tray carrying four small snuff boxes with red enamel lids. The room went really still.

I opened my box. Inside was a small white capsule.
Potassium cyanide.

Our very own poison tablets.

Thank you, Colonel!

The Colonel continued to talk in a hushed voice. "Keep this pill about your person at all times, and preferably sew it into your clothing. You never know when you might need it."

I turned the little box over. It has a hallmark on the back. Genuine silver. They spare no expense here. The only thing that comes cheap is human life.

Jakob P. Stromsheim

We are here, and we've spent our first night on Norwegian soil! I'm now inside a sleeping bag, inside a tent, on a hillside covered in snow somewhere or other on the Hardanger Plateau. But I'll start with the seconds just before my feet touched Norwegian snow.

I was dangling half out of the bomber, in the freezing night air. My arms ached because I was trying to hold on to the hatch while the wind tugged at my legs, and the whole aeroplane – it had suddenly slowed right down for the drop – was vibrating wildly. Three hundred metres below me lay a jumble of snowy hills and lakes and rocks and streams.

This was sheer madness.

But then, over the roar of the engines, I heard the words:

"Number one! GO!"

I dropped down into the freezing, moonlit sky. It was such a fast, clean fall. But after a few metres – and they passed in a trice – my parachute opened with a great jerk, and, for a moment, I was hoisted back upwards.

Then everything slowed down and I drifted towards the ground with the wind tearing at me all the time. The plane had done a loop and the sound of the engines died away as it headed back to Scotland.

Dotted around in the moonlight, were Lars, Åse and Freddie, all dressed in the same crinkly white camouflage suits as me, and all floating down in their parachutes. Further away still, there were twelve more, smaller parachutes. These were tied to twelve metal boxes containing all our stores and equipment. The boxes were coffin-shaped – one of Sergeant Sneydy's little jokes, I suppose. Maybe he thought a few coffins would come in handy.

When I first saw Norway from the plane, the Hardanger looked all smooth and white and flat. But now I could see that it wasn't flat at all. And the wind was pushing me towards the side of a very steep hill with huge boulders sticking out through the snow. The slope came towards me dead fast. I tried to steer the parachute away from the rocks. I bent my legs and crouched over.

Wham! Welcome to Norway.

I hit a huge hillock of snow and rolled to a stop. I'd missed the rocks and the landing had been painless. But, when I tried to get to my feet, I realized I was waist high in soft snow.

The parachute gave a sharp tug.

Help!

Quickly, before the wind could pull me down the hillside, I undid the cords, crumpled the parachute into a big ball and wedged it under the corner of a large rock.

Then I tried to get my bearings. It was a clear night, and I knew immediately that the navigator had got it wrong. We were definitely not in the Skoland marshes (which had been the plan). In the moonlight, I could see that I was in a long, steep valley with a lake (probably frozen over) at the foot. Gusts of snow-filled wind were scurrying everywhere. In the distance I could make out two white figures, one of them probably Åse to judge by the size, moving slowly towards each other.

I looked around to check none of the containers had fallen nearby, then, as I'd be walking into the wind, I put my head down and set out along the hillside to join them. The snow was so deep that I was wading rather than walking.

When I reached Lars and Åse, Freddie had already arrived with a large metal box that he'd tugged down the hill. The wind was too loud for anyone to hear anything, but I pointed to a huge boulder further down the slope. The others followed.

When we were in the lee of the boulder and out of the wind, we gathered round Freddie's metal box. It was smaller than the others (but still coffin-shaped) and had a red stripe down the side. This was Sergeant Sneyd's idea. It was an "overnight" container holding the things we'd need immediately after the drop.

And goodness, I'm grateful to him now.

Freddie undid the clasp and inside we found a spade, four sleeping bags, matches, a candle, a tiny primus stove, a saucepan, a loaf of pemmican, a bag of oats and – this was a surprise – a bag of sticky yellow crumbs.

"Aha!" said Freddie. He stuck his finger into the bag and licked it. He'd taste anything – even if it said POISON on the front, he'd still lick it.

"Lemon bonbons!" announced Freddie. "They must be from Mrs Collins."

We all stuck our fingers in the bag. The sticky lemon sugar tasted better than anything you can imagine.

Åse grimaced. "Says it all, doesn't it? Mrs C gives us lemon bonbons. And what does the Colonel give us? Poison capsules!"

After that, I sent Lars off to reconnoitre the valley – he said it felt familiar, but he couldn't be sure because it was so dark. Meanwhile I lit the primus stove and Freddie prepared something to eat. Åse took the spade and began digging a sleeping trench just under the boulder.

Lars returned a few minutes later. He'd worked out exactly where we were.

"We've been put down about thirty kilometres too far west. Ronsen's hut is further down this valley. That should be safe. It's a good weatherproof little shack.

And old Ronsen used to keep it well supplied."

"How far?" I asked. I'd never heard Lars say so much at once.

"It's a good day's journey," he replied. "And we'll have all the stuff to take with us."

That didn't sound good. We still had to find the other boxes and that could take us a long time. Even if it didn't snow overnight, the wind might cover them with snow. It was worrying, but I didn't say anything to the others.

Freddie had made porridge from melted snow and oats, with a sprinkling of lemon bonbon bits on top. We all hunkered around the stove and ate the mixture straight from the saucepan. I'm not sure that lemon-flavoured porridge was such a good idea, but at least it was hot and sweet.

Afterwards we carefully shook the snow from our camouflage suits, took off our boots, and wriggled into the sleeping bags. Even though we were going to sleep in all our clothes and our balaclavas, it would still be a very cold night.

The four of us lay close together: Freddie and me in the middle, Lars and Åse on either side. I tried to get as far down into my sleeping bag as possible, blowing on my hands and wriggling my toes to try and get warm. Then it occured to me that the arrangement wasn't quite right. Still in my sleeping bag, I got to my feet and jumped round till I was on the other side of Åse.

"Move along in," I said. "You go in the middle, Åse. You'll stay warmer."

"Excuse me?" said Åse.

"Quite right," added Freddie. "Åse, you can't be on the side. You have to have someone on either side to keep you warm. Little things get cold quicker. Your proportion of surface area to body mass is higher. That's why mice have fur and elephants only need skin."

"I'm not a mouse," huffed Åse.

"OK, Mouse," said Freddie.

"I said I'm NOT A MOUSE!"

"OK, Not-A-Mouse," said Freddie.

"Freddie, that's enough," I said. But I was smiling.

We settled down into our sleeping bags again and lay there, all huddled together. I tightened the sleeping bag drawstring round my face. Like the others, I had turned into a little pod of white material – with only my nose sticking out and a little cloud of breath emerging from my nostrils.

Dear God, please don't let it snow tonight! I thought.

I looked up. I had never been anywhere so wild at night. The sky was a vast arch of darkness, and it made me feel very small. We were just little specks of humanity about to set off on a huge, idiotically dangerous mission…

But there was no point thinking like that.

"The North star seems brighter here," I said.

"All the stars are brighter in Norway," replied Åse. "It's as if we're nearer to them."

And then Freddie told us about the stars. He showed us Aldebaran, and the double star Sirius, and the Seven Sisters of the Pleiades. He pointed out the belt of Orion the Hunter and the stars of his shoulder: Bellatrix and the red dwarf, Betelgeuse. On he went: Rigel, Saiph, Castor, Pollux… He was veering off into the minor nebulae when I finally dropped off to sleep.

Jakob P. Stromsheim

So here I am, writing this tucked up in the tent with the night closing in all around.

This morning I woke up with the sun in my face. It was so cold I didn't want to get up, but Lars was already crouched over the primus stove making tea. I wriggled out of my sleeping bag, cleaned my hands and face with some snow, and looked out across the valley.

The lake down below was white at the edges, but its centre glistened black where the water hadn't frozen. Along the valley bottom, skirting the edge of the lake, a thin band of birch trees swayed in the breeze. Nothing else seemed to live or move there.

The hillside we were perched on was jagged with boulders. As I'd feared, the wind had shifted the snow during the night. Somewhere, in among the boulders and crevices, the remaining eleven containers were now lying hidden.

We needed to find them. Quickly.

After breakfast I got Freddie to set up his signals equipment while the rest of us searched for the boxes. We each headed off in a different direction, trudging through the heavy, damp snow, all the while scanning the hillside for coffin-shaped lumps. Often what I thought was a box turned out to be just a rock or a lump in the snow. And when I did find a box, I usually tripped over it before I saw the metal edges sticking out through the snow.

By lunchtime we'd retrieved ten of the eleven coffins. But it was only in the late afternoon that Lars found the final box of ski equipment, wedged behind a small hillock down by the lakeside.

By that time it was too late to set out for the day, so we put up our two tents and I checked the contents of the last container. My stomach was churning with fear. I'd carefully gone through everything, so I immediately knew what was wrong. The spare tins of paraffin hadn't been packed. After tonight we'd have no more fuel.

We lit the stove, took off our soaking socks and boots and placed them as near as we could to the flame. Then, exhausted from our search, we got into our sleeping bags and huddled together.

Freddie made supper. He crumbled a loaf of pemmican into a biscuit box and added some oatmeal and water. Then he patted the mixture into balls and plopped them into the frying pan with a little butter. He called them "rissoles alla Hardanger".

As the rissoles began to crackle in the fat, I watched two small ducks fly down on to the lake. They sat low in the water.

Lars clicked his tongue.

"What's up?" I said.

"Those are black-throated divers. They shouldn't be here at this time of year."

"Is the weather too warm, then?" asked Åse.

Lars nodded. "It's made the snow sticky, and most of the lakes won't be safe to cross."

"I'm afraid we've no choice," I said. "We can't go over the mountains now, not without paraffin. We'll have to keep to the low ground where we can gather firewood."

The rissoles were ready and we picked them up with our gloves, and ate them straight from the pan. Then we spread out our map of the Hardanger Plateau on an undersheet and Lars pointed out where we were now and where, as far as he could remember, we'd find all the different mountain huts that were scattered over the plateau.

With advice from Lars, I planned out our route. We'd go along the edge of a long winding fjord, up over a mountain and down again, into the Skoland marshes, where we should have landed all along. Once we were on the far side of the marshes we'd make our way on to an upland area and then over the mountains to the last hut – the Fjosbudalen hut.

Then we'd be five kilometres from Vemork. It would be a long trek. I'd worked out that the last part of the journey on the uplands could take at least a week. Without fuel and with the ground boggy underfoot, I wasn't at all sure we'd make it with enough food left for the escape to Sweden.

But we did at least seem to be quite safe from Germans up here. I mentioned this to Lars, who nodded grimly.

"You're right," he said. "Nobody in their right mind comes here in winter." But then, in the kind of quiet voice that fills you with dread, he added, "It's the weather that'll be our real enemy."

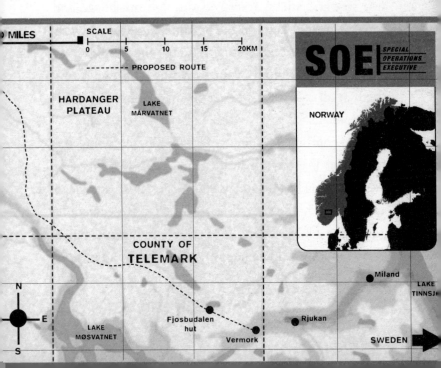

Jakob P. Stromsheim

I woke everyone just before dawn. Once we'd buried the primus stove – it'd be no good to us now – we set off down the mountainside.

We're not bad skiers, but the slope was steep and rocky and the backpacks were so heavy it took us a moment to get our balance. When we reached the lake we left our rucksacks, climbed up the mountain again, picked up the remaining packs and skied back down the hill a second time.

Then we set off along the lakeside. The snow was soft and sticky. It soaked through our boots, and formed great clumps on the bottoms of our skis. Every few minutes we had to stop to scrape the snow off. It's really awkward wiping your own skis. You can't reach them at all easily – it's like a fat man trying to cut his own toenails.

We continued along the lakeside, carrying the rucksacks in relay: forward and back, forward and back. It was a beautiful day. The air felt crisp and clean and the snow shone so brightly that it seemed to give off a bluish-white light. But I didn't pay much attention to this. I just kept my head down and pushed along on my ski poles as fast as I could. We had to reach Ronsen's hut in daylight. If the weather broke we wouldn't survive the night in the open.

The afternoon stretched out into early evening and still there was no sign of the hut.

Mindlessly I carried on pulling myself forward. I was completely exhausted, and my only thought was that we should do another stint before we tried to hunker down for another night in the open.

And then, as the trail wound around a shoulder of the mountain, a little brown hut came into view.

It looked tiny, tucked in among a glade of birch trees, but the sight of it made us quicken our pace. As we got nearer, the hut began to look a little bigger – but not very much bigger. When we arrived we realized it was barely the size of a child's Wendy house.

I lifted up the door latch and stooped inside. The smell reminded me of my grandfather's potting shed in Bergen – all earthy and damp.

I sent Lars down to the lake to collect water while the rest of us gathered firewood. I was piling up damp birch branches at the door when Åse came running towards me. She was puffing and bright-eyed.

"There's another little shed beyond the trees!" she cried.

"What's in it?"

"Guess," she said excitedly. I could see that it must be something very special. So could Freddie.

"Bottled blueberries?" he suggested.

"No. Better than that."

"Firelighters?" I asked, looking at our sodden firewood.

"No. Better still. Come and have a look!"

She scampered round the back of the hut and up into the trees. We followed and found her standing triumphantly beside a collapsing outhouse. At her feet, still half-wrapped in tarpaulin, was a large, sturdy-looking toboggan with metal runners.

What a relief! There would be no more going back and forth with the rucksacks. This would cut our journey time by *two-thirds*!

"I didn't tell you, but it's my birthday today," I said.

"And you couldn't have given me a better present."

Åse beamed with pleasure.

"I'll make you my birthday special, Jakob," added Freddie.

"What's that?" I asked, taken by surprise.

"Marmite flapjacks."

After supper, Freddie cooked his flapjacks. They were black and gave off a horrid acrid smell. I shut my eyes, put one in my mouth and bit into it. I just about managed to stop my face from puckering up, but my eyes watered. The taste was vile, the gritty little particles clinging to my teeth like barnacles. After the awful foot licking during the Colonel's interrogation, this was the nastiest thing I'd ever tasted.

Freddie offered the tin to the others. Lars shook his head, but Åse popped a square into her mouth. Almost immediately, she wriggled out of her sleeping bag and bolted for the door.

I heard retching noises from outside the hut.

"I knew you'd like them," said Freddie confidently. "So many things are improved by a spot of Marmite: meringues, fairy cakes, boiled carrots. Now if only I had a little tube of anchovy paste…"

Åse returned, wiping her mouth against the back of her hand. "We could use those as weapons against the Germans," she said. I pretended to be studying the map and somehow managed to keep a straight face.

Freddie gave her a disappointed look.

When we'd banked up the fire for the night I arranged all the food supplies in neat piles on the floor of the hut. I had to calculate rations. It would be three weeks until the raid – though that could always change – and then there would be ten more days for the journey into Sweden. I also needed some reserves for emergencies. I did some sums in my head, then took a plate and measured out: one cup of oatmeal; one cup of flour; one loaf of pemmican; twelve biscuits; a piece of cheese about the size of a pack of playing cards; half a pack of butter; and four squares of chocolate.

"Is that breakfast?" asked Freddie.

"Nope, that's the daily rations."

He gave me a crestfallen look. His hand crept towards the chocolate. I slapped it back quickly.

"I don't know if even I could eat a whole loaf of pemmican every day," he grumbled.

"This is the daily ration for *all of us*," I replied. "I thought you were meant to be brilliant at maths?"

He looked astonished.

"But that wouldn't feed a mouse," he protested, looking at Åse.

"Don't start that again. I'm NOT a mouse!" said Åse.

But Freddie was right. It *is* a pitifully small amount of food, especially when we are going to be out in the cold, skiing all day long.

I'm not sure the others realize, but things look very bad. How are we going to keep our strength up?

It's time to settle in for the night, so I've put the food away. There's nothing to do now but huddle further into our sleeping bags. It's so good to be warm at last and out of the wind. I was just lying here with a lovely sleepy heaviness descending on me, when I got that burnt Marmite taste at the back of my mouth.

Note to self: keep an eye on Freddie's cooking.

Jakob P. Stromsheim

15TH DECEMBER 1942

Several days have passed, but there's not been much to write about because every day seems the same.

But let me go back to that first morning when we were staying in our tiny hut.

We rose just before dawn. Lars rubbed a candle along the runners of the toboggan and Åse looped some rope around one of the bars to make a harness. Right at the last moment, I decided that there was no point taking the tents – they were heavy and cumbersome and slowed us down. Of course *not* having them would mean that if a storm blew up suddenly, we'd be caught short. But that was a risk I was going to have to take. Compared with some of the other risks we were facing, it really didn't amount to much.

Nobody argued with my decision and soon we set out along the lakeside, with Lars at the back pulling the toboggan along like a big, silent ox. Slowly the light crept up over the mountains and, after the mist rose from the lake, we found ourselves in bright, cold sunshine.

We forged ahead, pushing our poles through the sticky snow, trying to ignore the damp creeping into our boots and up our legs. In places the face of the mountain was so steep it felt as though the rock and snow towering over us would come crashing down at any moment. We skied on as fast as we could.

Our pace was much better, thanks to the toboggan, and soon the tiny hut disappeared behind us. As the morning wore on, the landscape altered, the mountains becoming less steep and the fjord widening out into a series of inlets, like the fingers of a hand. In colder weather we would have skied straight across these stretches of water, but the ice was still too thin. Instead we skirted around the edges and, occasionally, when we came across level ground, we raced each other to the next clump of trees or big rock.

Lars always won, but it was still great fun. At one

point I even thought, *Goodness, I'm enjoying this. Maybe everything isn't quite so impossible after all.*

Most of the time we were skiing downhill, so we were making better time. I worried whether we were pushing our luck with no tent, but Lars had said we'd come to a hut before the end of the day. I kept scanning the sides of the fjord, but no buildings came into view. Finally, just as dusk was beginning to fall, I spotted something barely bigger than a Monopoly piece. It was another little brown hut!

When we reached the hut we gathered up birch branches and, after much blowing and fiddling, we lit a slow, smoky fire. Then we ate, curled ourselves up in our sleeping bags and went to sleep.

And this – with better and worse fires, and better or worse food (depending on how well supplied the hut is), is how we've spent the last few nights. We ski until late afternoon and then we come to a hut. Some are barely more than hovels filled with animal droppings, others are neat, trim, little chalets with shutters and verandas and tins of food in the cupboards.

The day before yesterday we came to the head of the fjord and began a slow climb out of the valley, leaving the trees and the fjord behind. We followed a small, icy-cold river up on to the higher land. The ascent was hard work – we'd gathered bundles of branches for

121

firewood and had tied them on to the toboggan. We now took it in turns to pull the load along.

Finally, we came out on the top of the plateau. Here was a pure, bare world of rock and snow. There were dips and rises in the land, but the whiteness seemed to stretch out for ever.

At first our main guide was the river. Then, as time passed, the river became smaller and smaller. Eventually it disappeared completely.

After that, we were on our own, just us and our compasses. It was impossible to know for sure exactly where we were. We scrutinized the map, trying to follow each contour, and we held up our compasses every few minutes to check we were still heading four degrees south-east to where the Grasfell marshes lay.

For two whole days we've continued on through this blank, white land. The weather has been eerily good – with clear skies and just a light breeze. And every evening Lars says how lucky we are and that there must be a cold front soon. (Åse rolls her eyes at this.)

But each morning we wake up to more clear skies and we set off again across the great white desert. Nothing changes from one hour to the next. And with so little for the mind to latch on to, I am becoming hyper observant (and hyper bored and hyper boring!).

I seem to notice every large rock or strange-shaped cloud, or hovering bird.

We've passed the tracks of wild sheep and once we even saw a mountain hare, but there have been no ski tracks, no signs of people. In the huts we stay in it's been clear that no one has visited recently. Why would they? There's nothing here but snow and ice and emptiness. We might as well be on the moon.

DLIFE OF THE HARDANGER PLATEAU

following wildlife can be found on the Hardanger
eau. If there is wildlife in the area, you will be able
identify it by studying the paw prints.

REINDEER	
PINE MARTEN	
FOX	
ARCTIC FOX	
HARE	
LYNX	
WOLVERINE	
LEMMING	

WILDLIFE OF THE HARDANGER PLATEAU

FIG 2: REINDEER ON THE HARDANGER

Jakob P. Stromsheim

You remember me writing yesterday that the weather was "eerily good"? Well, today I'm lucky to be alive! This is what happened.

It was our third day on the high plateau, and we were making our way down to the Grasfell marshes when the weather finally broke.

It happened very quickly, in a matter of minutes. The sky suddenly grew overcast, as if a shadow had passed in front of the sun, and a cold westerly wind whipped up the loose snow all around us. I stopped and tightened my hood, adjusted my goggles and then, head down, I went on down the slope. There was a mountain hut about 200 metres away, over a stretch of flat ice. If we could reach it, we could rest up until things improved.

At the foot of the slope I stopped and waited for Åse, who was a few metres behind me. Lars and Freddie were further back, manoeuvring the toboggan (my birthday present had proved to be a blessing *and* a curse). I couldn't call out – the wind was too loud – so instead, I pointed with my ski pole across the ice in front of me. I knew that there, under the snow and ice, lay a mountain pool.

If it had been calm, with the sun shining, I would have skirted round the side – I could see clumps of snow-covered reeds marking the edges. But I was in a hurry. We had to get to that hut as quickly as possible.

With my head down against the wind, I set out. The ice was covered in a thick layer of wet snow that slushed up round my boots.

I hadn't gone more than five metres when I heard what I took to be the crack of a rifle. Then more shots – really one strange, long, drawn-out shot – rang out. I stopped and looked round. I could just make out Åse back at the edge of the ice. Her arms were in the air, waving frantically, but I had no idea why.

All of a sudden I did know why. The surface gave way beneath my feet. I crashed down through the ice. And water *so cold* closed over my head.

I opened my eyes – the shock had pulled my breath away and bubbles were churning out of my mouth. I was going down into the blackness. I pulled my goggles down and flailed my arms around and kicked with my legs. But my skis were still attached to my boots and the weight was dragging me down.

I unclipped my skis and kicked harder. With a gasp I reached the surface. I grabbed at the edge of the ice and started to hoist myself up, but the ice crumbled under my weight and I was pulled back down again.

This time I couldn't get to the surface. The rucksack on my back had become waterlogged and was pulling me down. I wriggled free of the straps and came up for air. The rucksack, which contained half our food supplies, sank immediately.

My skis were floating by my side and I thought clearly enough to fling them up on to the surface of the lake towards the shore. I grabbed at the slippery edge of the ice again but again the ice gave way beneath me.

I knew the science. Only a minute more and then my heart would stop. Already I was getting weirdly sleepy.

Then above the wind came the sound of a voice.

"Jakob! Here! Here!"

It was Åse.

She flung a rope towards me. I reached out to grab it, but my movements were slow and fumbling and the rope somehow just slipped by me. Åse hauled the rope back towards herself ready to throw it again.

The cold and tiredness were pressing down on me now and everything seemed to be happening so slowly. Åse threw the rope again. This time I grabbed hold of it through my soaking gloves and Åse began to pull.

But it all went wrong. Åse started to slide across the ice towards me. I was pulling her out onto the lake.

Then came a hard jerk on the rope. Lars had caught

up with Åse and was pulling as well. With a great sucking noise, I was plucked out of the water and pulled along the ice.

A little way from the side I let go of the rope and scrambled on to all fours. If I stood up I might well go through the ice again. I crawled back to the bank.

Lars grabbed me and dragged me to my feet. The water had been freezing, but the wind was even worse. It blew straight through my soaking clothes, chilling every part of me.

"Get his clothes off or he'll freeze," Lars shouted out over the wind.

"The food was in that rucksack, wasn't it?" yelled Freddie.

"Shut up and help!" cried Åse.

I stood there, limp and pathetic, as they stripped my clothes off me, underpants included. Åse looked away, but it didn't matter to me – I was beyond caring.

Once undressed they wrapped a blanket round me whilst they found a dry set of clothes for me to put on. There was nothing to be done about my boots – I had to put them back on soaking and waterlogged.

"Now jump!" Lars ordered.

Exhausted and half-dead with cold, I started to jump. My first jumps were pretty feeble. But I kept on. I jumped twenty jumps, then thirty more jumps – it seemed to work. I began to feel a little bit of warmth returning to my limbs.

By the time I'd done another thirty jumps, Åse had retrieved my skis from the ice and we had to get going again. (She's as light as a waterboatman and can probably walk on anything!)

Progress was slow, for the snow was thick as a blizzard and the wind was growing stronger by the minute. I couldn't see more than an arm's length in front of me. I kept pulling myself forward, and with the anorak hood pulled in tight, all I could see was the tunnel of swirling white in front of me.

The snow driving into my face froze to my skin immediately. And my nose was running, but I soon gave up trying to wipe it. The main thing was to get to that hut.

As I struggled along, I couldn't stop thinking about the food that had been in my rucksack and was now deep down in the bottom of the lake. Why hadn't I divided the food up and put a little in each pack? Why? Why? Why?

We didn't find the hut – it found us. Lars's skis bumped straight into the side wall with such force that he crumpled to the ground. He let out a shout and got back onto his feet. Then we blundered after him, feeling our way along the wall of the hut until we came to a little door, which was half-buried in a snowdrift.

Freddie took out the spade and started to dig – and the rest of us scrabbled away in our gloves. Eventually we wrestled the door open, and stumbled in from the storm. We brought the sled in with us, and banged the door shut.

The hut was very basic: a small window, a small, stone-lined stove, a table and four chairs. And that was it.

Everyone pulled off their goggles and Åse stared at me for a moment. Then she began to laugh. Then Freddie looked at me and he started to laugh too. Then I noticed that even Lars was smiling faintly.

What on earth was so funny?

I tried to smile too, but it hurt when I moved my mouth and my skin felt very peculiar and numb.

"You look like an elephant!" said Åse.

I put my hand up to my nose. A thick, tube-shaped icicle had formed on my nose and upper lip. I had a trunk!

"There's only one way to melt this," said Åse. She took off her gloves and pressed her bare hand up against my cheek, just at the root of the giant icicle. Lars did the same, while Freddie held my trunk and wobbled it gently to and fro.

Just for that moment, with my friends huddled round me, I managed to forget that the rucksack had gone and that our dinner was now food for the fish.

Åse Jeffries

17th December 1942

This hut is *really* shoddy. A huff and a puff and it should all come down. Amazingly, it hasn't – even though there's been a blizzard yowling like a herd of alley cats since we got here last night.

Maybe the hut stays up because it acts like a kind of sieve. There are so many little cracks in the planks that the wind just rips straight through. Jakob and I spent this morning tearing up bits of newspaper and stuffing them into the cracks, but it doesn't seem to have made much difference.

So I'm sitting here at the little table by the stove with my fingers black with newsprint and not only can I see my breath – I can see it *blow away* too. There is also water drip-drip-dripping down my neck from the ice on the ceiling that's been melting all day.

But hey! At least we're inside and not freezing to death. Jakob, apart from a slightly drippy nose and very red skin on his face (where his trunk was amputated), seems to have recovered completely from his little dip.

Thank goodness we had all that firewood on the toboggan! We've kept the hut well above freezing, but it's not *that* warm. We've spent the day in our sleeping bags (I've got mine on now). You quickly learn to shuffle around in them, and if we ever *do* make it back, we'll win all our school sack races.

We've also got entertainment – there are some old angling magazines, and Jakob has found a big ball of string and he's practising his knots with it. The string has other uses too. Lars has been binding a handle onto his combat knife to give it a better grip (the Colonel will be shocked to think of someone fiddling with the design).

And this morning, when I said I was going out for a pee (the boys have been using a bucket in the corner, but I thought I was above such things), Jakob tied a length of string round my waist. He tied the other end to the door post – which made me feel like a toddler out on reins for a shopping trip with mum.

Gee! He was right. Inside the hut you forget just how big and scary the storm outside is. I'd barely closed the door when the wind blew me flat on my face. I somehow managed to do my business (next time I'll use the pot, thank you), but the blizzard was so thick and white it was as if I was stuck in some giant vat of freezing mashed potato. I became completely confused and had to use the string to guide me back to the door. I've never been so pleased to see those three boys again in my life!

So that was my Near Death Experience for today. (There's sure to be another tomorrow.) The main problem we face now is that we don't really have anything to eat. When Jakob went down in the lake he took nearly half our supplies with him. (And I'm proud to say that I have managed to restrain myself and *not* yell at him for being so stupid as to divide up the food into only two bags.)

We still have more than two weeks before we head off to almost certain death at Vemork power station. And then, if by some freakish chance we *do* survive, we still have to get ourselves to Sweden – a trivial matter of 400 kilometres. That'll take about ten days. So while we're holed up here, we'll have to eat almost nothing.

Jakob, whose every second word at the moment

seems to be "sorry", has worked out our daily rations and there's not much to look forward to: a piece of cheese slightly smaller than a full-grown raisin every day, and a square of chocolate *every fourth day*.

We had a biscuit each for lunch – lunch! – and then Fred made a flour and pemmican stew for supper. The helpings were unbelievably small. It would have made an ant weep.

Åse Jeffries

Another day shut up in the hut. Today there were chocolate rations. I cut my square up into tiny slivers with a penknife. Then very, very slowly I ate it. One sliver at a time.

And that has been the big event of the day. There's not much else to report – the storm is too rough for the radio to work and Jakob is less snivelly than he was, but now he has a boil on his neck that looks like a mini Mount Etna.

And, of course, we're hungry. I always thought you were meant to feel light-headed and otherworldly when you don't eat. But surprise, surprise! We just feel hungry. I haven't been thinking about God and the Meaning of Life. I have relived every single meal Mrs Collins made – even her toad in the hole that didn't rise properly.

What should we do? Lie in our sleeping bags saving energy but getting unfit? Or keep moving about but use up our fat reserves? In the end your body decides for you. I can't be bothered to do anything…

I'm going to turn in now for the night. My fingers are too cold to write any more.

Åse Jeffries

Yet another day shut up in the hut. The blizzard is still belting away at full blast and the hunger is really beginning to get to me. Why did I agree to go on this mission? Why? Why? Why?

This morning I stood up too quickly, keeled straight over, and smashed my head against the stove. I've spent the rest of the day lying in my sleeping bag, unable to face the prospect of getting up. The others look pretty rough too. Fred's legs are swollen and he has to get up all the time in the night to pee. Jakob's boil is even redder than before. Only Lars seems OK, but even he isn't moving more than he absolutely has to.

All day we drop in and out of sleep. Hours pass with nothing except the occasional sigh or snuffle, or little bits of bickering about how and when to feed the firewood into the stove. Jakob has insisted that we ration our fuel and try to keep the stove just going and no more, because the storm could go on FOR EVER! (Lars says he remembers one that lasted ten days…)

On the plus side, all this lolling around is perfect for daydreaming. Here is my current list of things I want to happen *right now*:

1. I want the storm to stop and the sun to come out.

2. I want Jakob's gigantic boil to burst.

3. I want the war to end.

4. I want to find a giant Mrs Collins' lemon drizzle cake under the floorboards.

5. I want to go home.

Åse Jeffries

20TH DECEMBER 1942

Did we do something to offend the gods? This is day five and the storm has got *worse*. The wind is so strong that the hut quivers like a tent, and the screeching is not just ten alley cats, but a hundred, or a million.

Jakob's boil finally met its maker today. This morning I tried to lance it with a needle. But Jakob gave such a yelp and he wouldn't let me have a second go. I had to hold a little piece of mirror up (funny what you find in the cupboards here) while he did it himself. The gloop spurted out – a horrible explosion of pale custardy stuff. Really revolting.

I thought we were on a mission to save the world. Instead it turns out we're stuck in a freezing shed, prodding spots.

Åse Jeffries

Yet another day in the sleeping bag. We're all feeling rotten. Fred's legs are even more puffed up (his ankles seem to have completely disappeared). I can feel the glands in my neck and my muscle conditioning is completely shot. At the moment, I couldn't do a decent front hand spring on the vault if my life depended on it.

We're also running out of firewood. Lars was going to go out to see if he could find a woodpile, but there was so much snow piled up against the door, he couldn't even get out.

So we've done the only thing we could and chopped up the table. It's been burning nicely and we've spent the evening drinking hot water (you have to gulp it quickly because it cools down so fast) and lying here in our sleeping bags blethering on about our lives and remembering good meals we've had.

When I say "we", I mean Fred, Jakob and I. Lars never says anything, unless it's about the weather or the wood supplies. Jakob has told us about going clay pigeon shooting with his dad, Fred has explained the principles of light refraction and how to galvanize a zinc bucket, but Mr No-Chat has no chat. I've been cooped up in here for days with him, but I still know nothing about his parents, or his school, or his friends, or anything.

All I know is that Lars has a brother. This is how I found out:

I'd been talking about my little sister Trudie and how irritatingly perfect and blonde she is (of course I have to take after the dark-haired American side of the family). I was telling them how Trude never smudges her homework, never loses her gloves, always makes her bed and arranges her toys on her bedside table, blah-blah-blah-blah and how, despite all that, I really miss her.

As per usual Lars said nothing and just stared into the fire.

So I thought I'd push the boat out a little.

"Hey! Lars," I said. "Do you have any brothers or sisters?"

No reply.

"Lars, do you have any brothers or sisters?"

Nada.

"LARS!"

"Mmmmmm?" he said in his just-returning-from-Planet-Zog tone of voice.

"Do you have any brothers or sisters?"

"Yes," he said.

"A brother or a sister?" He makes you do all the running.

"A brother."

"Older or younger?"

"Older."

"How much older?"

"Eleven years." And then he went back to staring at the fire, with a "conversation over" look to him.

So I'm left wondering. What's the brother like? Is he fat or thin? Is he a champion tap dancer? Does he have a duelling scar down across one cheek? We will never know.

Åse Jeffries

22ND DECEMBER 1942

A chocolate day! Otherwise nearly nothing to eat. Any food is OK if you are absolutely starving. Fred says some of the Eskimos in Alaska are very partial to the little yellow gadfly grubs they find in the nostrils of the caribou – and they eat them alive. I would eat anything now, even wriggling caribou-snot-covered little grubs.

In fact we could eat more, but Jakob has carefully set rations aside for the journey into Sweden. And, maddeningly, he won't be talked out of it.

Jakob likes everything oh-*so*-neat-and-tidy. Even his fires! This morning, when I opened the stove and chucked a piece of skirting board in (we'll burn anything here) he gave me this pained, in-sorrow-rather-than-anger look.

I glared back at him.

"Åse, all I'm asking is that you don't just throw the wood in the stove – place it carefully. We can't afford to waste it."

"That's ridiculous!" I said.

But Jakob had on his extra-patient, grown-up-talking-to-a-three-year-old voice. "If you put the wood in at the front like that it blocks off all the heat. The middle of the fire is the hottest bit where those nice red embers are."

"For heaven's sake! It'll burn anyway." He's such a fusspot.

"Listen, Mouse," he said.

"Don't you *dare* call me Mouse!"

He backed off.

But then of course Fred had to wade in. "It's interesting you should think that red is so hot. In fact the most intensely exothermic parts of a fire aren't normally red. Of the colours visible to the human eye red indicates the coolest temperature and violet the hottest. Astronomers can look at the colours and can work out the temperature of stars by—"

"SHUT UP!" yelled Jakob, Lars and I all at once.

And, just for once, he did.

We've started burning the chairs – there were four of them and we're already breaking up chair number two. It was a choice: burn 'em, or eat 'em.

Åse Jeffries

23RD DECEMBER 1942

The storm is over. Last night the din of the million yowling alley cats died down to a *whooshing* noise – as if the hut was just by the side of a huge waterfall. By morning there was no sound at all.

The door was completely blocked by snow, so we had to climb out of the window and dig down to the door. Once we stepped outside, we found ourselves in a very weird landscape.

You know when you're at a smart restaurant and you're bored out of your mind and the hot wax is dribbling down the candles and you mould it into strange shapes? Well, the wind had done just that with the snow, piling it against rocks and then hollowing it out in the most peculiar ways. Now there are strange pinnacles and swirls and mounds everywhere. One of the protuberances looks just like Colonel Armstrong's beaky nose.

I took a brief walk round the outside of the hut to see if my legs were still working after all those days in the sleeping bag. I forced Fred to come with me – I think part of the problem with his legs is that he hasn't been moving much.

When we went back inside the hut, the stink of bodies and stale air really hit me. We'd been cooped up for so long we hadn't noticed the fug.

Fred has been trying to get the radio to work all day. With the storm over, the signal shouldn't have been too hard to get, but the accumulators are short of acid so the batteries can't work properly. The generator is also a nightmare. It has to be wound by hand and, unless you're a fifty-tonne sumo wrestler, that's pretty hard going. Jakob now has blisters all over both hands.

Lars has hacked away at the snowdrifts round the hut and found a small wood pile, so for the moment we won't have to burn the two remaining chairs. He's also come up with a new source of food. This morning he dug down to some rocks and uncovered this greyish-looking spiky lichen called reindeer moss. We boiled it up with some oatmeal for lunch.

The moss is meant to be full of vitamins. It's OK to put in your mouth – the consistency is a bit like wet sand – but you have to think hard about something else if you ever want to swallow it.

We had a discussion about food this afternoon. I told Jakob if we didn't increase our rations we wouldn't be strong enough for the mission and – whoopee! – he agreed.

So he's going to use up some of our emergency supply and tonight we'll be doubling the rations – we'll have half a loaf of pemmican each. And tomorrow Lars and Jakob are going out with their guns to hunt for reindeer. If they don't catch something quickly we will all starve to death. I'd been hoping for a rather more dramatic ending – a shoot-out or a massive explosion. Anything but this slow misery.

Åse Jeffries

Lars and Jakob set off at dawn this morning. The extra food – and maybe that awful reindeer moss – has made all the difference. Fred's legs have gone down a bit, Jakob is looking better and I've felt well enough to spend most of today out of my sleeping bag.

More reindeer moss for lunch. Yeuch! Still, it was better than Fred's Marmite flapjacks. He hasn't noticed yet, but I've hidden his Marmite in the bag with the fuses and rubber gloves. It was a mean thing to do, but I just can't bear the smell of that stuff any more.

This afternoon I've been checking over the explosives, counting out the charges and looking at the plans. Every three minutes I go to the window just to see if there's any sight of Jakob and Lars. In my mind's eye I've already got those venison steaks sizzling in the pot. If the boys come back empty-handed, I'll eat one of them instead – though Lars might be a bit tough and stringy.

Fred had been fiddling with his transmitter for most of the morning without much luck. And then suddenly, at 3.00 p.m. he got through to London.

Tap-tappity-tap-tap-tap.

He tapped on for some time, explaining that we hadn't been in contact earlier because of the storm. There were taps back from London. Then more tapping from Fred. Then a long pause. When London's message eventually came in, I heard Fred curse under his breath. When he tapped his reply he was really walloping the telegraph key.

"What's the problem?" I asked.

"Look," said Fred. "This is what they sent me!" He handed me the scrap of paper where he'd been scrawling down the Morse. The note said: WHAT DID YOU SEE WALKING DOWN THE STRAND IN THE EARLY HOURS OF JANUARY I 1941?

"I always thought the signals people were a bit strange," I said.

"Everybody taps their Morse slightly differently and they recognize us by how we tap," Fred explained. "My fingers are so stiff from the cold that they must have thought I was a fake. So they're checking up."

"And what did you tap back?"

"Three pink elephants."

"What?"

"That's the password we agreed at Drumincraig."

"And what did the operator reply?"

Fred grinned. "Congratulations. A baby brother, Einar. Red hair. Looks just like you did."

I'd say one Freddie is quite enough, thank you!

Jakob P. Stromsheim

29TH DECEMBER 1942

Åse gave me the log five days ago, but I haven't really had the strength to write. I've felt so wretched. But now I'll go back to the day after the storm ended.

On that first day Lars and I didn't find any reindeer. We came back to a dreadful evening in the hut where we were all so miserable we barely talked at all. We went out again the next day – Christmas Day, which we had decided to ignore – and the next day, and the day after, and the day after that. And each day, from first light until nightfall, we made our way over this vast, lonely plateau. By nightfall we were nearly delirious with hunger and exhaustion. We *had* to find something.

But there were no reindeer.

Then this morning – our sixth day of hunting – the temperature dropped to minus twenty degrees. We were huddled round the stove having our porridge when gunfire rang out across the plateau.

Were we being attacked? Åse, Freddie and

I stumbled out of our sleeping bags and ran to the door, but Lars called us back. Nobody was shooting anything – it was the sound of the ice cracking away from the land.

Lars and I left the hut just after dawn (much later than it sounds in a Norwegian winter) and skied north-west, with a bitter wind on our backs. At mid-morning we stopped on the brow of a hill and, for the hundredth millionth time, we picked up our binoculars and scanned the horizon.

Far away, on the ridge of a hill, I saw some small black specks. My heart gave a jolt.

Reindeer at last!

But Lars gripped me by the arm. "Stay very still," he whispered. "No sudden movements. No noise. Reindeer can't see well, but their ears are very sharp. And they can smell *anything*. Follow me."

Slowly and carefully we skied downhill, using the ridges and hollows in the mountainside as cover. By the time we reached the bottom of the valley the reindeer had disappeared over the horizon. Lars crouched down to examine the tracks. There were scuff marks where the reindeer had been lying and the ground was churned up where they'd been grazing.

"They're heading north into the wind," said Lars. "They won't change direction unless they're startled and they're not moving fast – maybe four or five kilometres an hour. We should catch up with them on the lakeside by midday."

We set off again, not following the reindeer directly, but forking off down a parallel valley so as to keep a hillside between us and them.

We travelled on for about eight kilometres, gliding along the side of the hills, using the occasional dip in the ground to peer over and check on the herd. As we got closer to the lakeside, I caught the occasional glimpse of antlers, like tiny moving trees.

When we came level with the herd, we stopped,

took off our skis, and stuck them upright in the ground. Carrying the rifles on our backs, we quietly crawled up to the summit and looked over.

Hurrah!

There, in the valley below, seventy or eighty reindeer were scattered across the land. Some were grazing, while others were lying on the ice (their coats must be very warm) chewing the cud.

Beautiful creatures. And delicious. All that food just lying there for the taking…

But there was a problem. They were out of range. And we couldn't get any closer without breaking cover. Neither could we tuck round northwards and approach from the other side because we'd be upwind and the reindeer would pick up our scent and bolt.

We were stuck. All we could do was sit it out and hope that they came to us.

We hunkered down and waited.

I felt desperate. I was so cold and hungry and I knew we had to shoot a reindeer or we'd never have the strength to complete the mission. I willed the reindeer to climb the hill towards us. *Come this way. Lots of lovely reindeer moss up here. Come on, come on…*

The reindeer didn't budge.

We waited and waited. Below us, more of the herd were starting to lie down on the ice. I looked at my watch. It was twelve thirty – which meant there was less than three hours of daylight left.

Then Lars nudged me. Down below us two young bucks had separated themselves from the herd and were making their way up the hill. They stopped at a patch of higher ground, dug out the snow with their hooves and started to graze.

Lars pointed to a small mound below. From there the young bulls would be within shooting range. Lars moved as stealthily as a fox and I copied him. Very carefully I got to my feet and started to edge down the mountainside, keeping my eyes trained on the reindeer.

Halfway down to the mound, we came to a patch of ice on the slope, and just at that moment one of the bucks raised its head and turned towards us. We stopped dead.

We were dressed in white and a reindeer's eyesight is poor. If we kept still he might mistake us for part of the hillside.

The other buck looked up. Two huge pairs of eyes stared at us.

A long, still moment followed. I held my breath.

The ice was slippery and I tried not to wobble, but my right foot lost its hold and I came crashing down on the ice.

The bucks stamped the ground with their hind legs and bolted down the hillside with a flurry of snow. In a moment the whole herd was up and away over the brow of the hill.

That was it – our chance was gone.

"I'm sorry," I said.

Lars's face was expressionless. "They didn't pick up a scent, so they may not have gone far," he said. "We must get a move on. We haven't long before the light goes."

We set off again after the reindeer. And Lars's guess – thank goodness! – was soon proved right. The herd had only moved to the next valley.

The terrain there was more uneven, with plenty of rocks and hollows in the ground that made for good cover. But the reindeer were now more restless. And so was the wind – it seemed to be continually changing direction. This was dangerous. It meant that the reindeer could pick up our scent at any moment.

We crept forward, guns at the ready. When we got to about 200 metres from the herd we could see the reindeers' breath, which meant we were close enough to shoot.

Lars crouched behind a rock and I took up position in the shadow of a nearby hillock.

We would aim at the reindeers' chests, not their heads. Lars had told me that a reindeer shot in the diaphragm doesn't usually collapse suddenly, thus frightening the herd. Instead the animal will often

stand still for a minute and then slowly crumple to the ground. With a bit of luck, the other reindeer would mistake the gunshot for the sound of cracking ice and continue to graze. This would give us chance to shoot another animal before the herd stampeded.

That, at least, was the theory. We aimed and shot at just the same time. Instantly, in a flash of speed, the entire herd thundered off up the hillside.

Lars fired two shots after them, but a second later the herd was over the brow of the hill. There was nothing left but a large patch of scuffed snow.

I groaned.

Lars walked over to where the reindeer had been grazing.

Suddenly I felt cold and tired. "Let's go," I said. "We've lost them for good now."

"Wait! Look!" Lars pointed to the ground.

There were drops of blood in the snow.

"Quick!" he said. And we half ran, half stumbled up the mountainside, following the red trail.

A little way beyond the summit we found a young female reindeer. She was lying on the ground, her feet scrabbling against the snow as she struggled to get back on her feet. Lars stopped and fired a shot. The reindeer slumped down dead, blood pouring from her head.

Lars took a small enamel cup from his backpack, held it up to the reindeer's head and collected the blood pouring from the wound.

He took a gulp and then passed me the steaming cup.

Just for a second, I blanched. Then I closed my eyes, put the cup to my lips and drank. The blood had a slightly metallic taste, which reminded me of a particularly horrible nosebleed I once had, but I cast that thought from my mind and swallowed some more. And as the blood warmed me up, I did begin to feel a bit better.

We drank a second cupful, and then a third. Soon the strange dizziness I'd been feeling all afternoon had gone.

Next Lars took his knife from his pack and prised a small bone out of the foot of the reindeer. He snapped it in two and drank the clear liquid inside.

He passed me another bone. "Marrow. Try it. Do you good."

This time I didn't even pause. I took the bone, cracked it and sucked up the liquid inside.

After that, we butchered the rest of the carcass. You could see Lars had done this before – he worked so fast.

First he skinned the animal and laid the hide on the snow. Then, with several big blows, he chopped the head off and tossed it to me.

"Cut the tongue out, we'll eat that tonight."

I opened the jaw as wide as I could and sawed through the flesh. The poor reindeer stared up at me like a patient at the dentist.

Meanwhile Lars slit open the belly and delved inside. I thought he might throw away the innards, but instead he took out the heart, kidneys, stomach and a huge dark red organ that flopped and slithered as he laid it on the hide.

"The liver," said Lars. "Want a bit now?"

I shook my head. I was hungry, but not *that* hungry.

We wrapped up the organs and the meat in the hide (I could see now why he started off by skinning the reindeer – it acted as our shopping bag) and tied the leg bones together in a bundle. Then we went back down the valley and put our skis on again.

It was only now that I noticed how our shadows had lengthened. With all the excitement, the butchery and the blood-drinking, I'd lost track of time. It was getting late and we were going to have to race home against the setting sun.

"It'll take ages if we go back the way we came," said Lars.

"Let's try cutting across south-east," I suggested. "That way we should come out by the lakeside."

Lars nodded. He handed me a strip of reindeer fat to chew on and we set off across the slope.

Despite the added weight of the reindeer, we skied fast, but, coming down a sharp incline, I took a corner too fast, and lost my balance.

I tumbled down the slope and crashed to a halt with something very hard jammed against the small of my back.

I lay there dazed, not knowing whether my head or my back hurt the most. But nothing was broken. Lars came and helped me to my feet and, after I'd shaken myself down, we skied on.

Eight kilometres further on we stopped beside a small waterfall. It was getting darker and by now we should have reached the summit where we first saw the reindeer.

I turned to Lars. "Well?"

He took off his balaclava and shook his head. "I'm sorry. I just don't recognize this place."

It was time to check our bearings. I felt in my pocket for the compass. The pocket was empty. I looked again. No compass. I tried my left-hand pocket, though I knew perfectly well that I never put anything in there.

Lars watched me stolidly.

I tried my back pockets and then I started patting myself all over, feeling faintly sick. I must have lost the compass during that fall. How stupid. Now we were *really* lost.

"Don't worry," said Lars. Taking out his penknife, he pulled back his anorak, and cut off a little brown button that was sewn into a seam.

He handed the button to me. Suddenly I knew exactly what it was and I gave a little yelp of recognition.

"My father had one of these!" I cried.

The button was made of plastic. It was such a pleasing thing – it had a nice weight to it and it was warm and pleasant to hold. The shape fitted perfectly into the palm of my hand. It was also not what it first seemed. I turned the button over. On the back, inside a bubble of liquid, was the tiny dial and the settings of a hidden compass.

"My father called this his 'secret device'," I said to Lars. "He kept it in his flying jacket. He says he was given it by some chap at the War Office. He liked it better than any of his medals and—"

Something stopped me in my tracks.

I looked more closely at the button, tilting it slightly to one side and then the other.

This was impossible!

I looked again.

Scratched into the side of the button, in neat capitals, were the initials A.S.

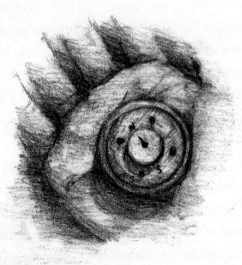

My father, Ansfrid Stromsheim, has always been a meticulous man. He labels everything – socks, underwear, screwdrivers ... everything. These were his initials. This was *his* button.

It came from some secret unit within the war department where the officials wear Homburg hats and wouldn't tell Father their surnames or where they lived. In fact, Father told me he shouldn't have shown the button to anyone at all. But he did. And this was quite definitely his button.

I stared at Lars. How on earth did the button land up with him?

"This was my father's button. Look, his initials are here on the side. Where did you find it, Lars?"

Lars took a long sniff and looked at the ground. When he spoke, he did so carefully, picking his words as if each one was a wobbly stepping stone.

"I found it ... in a wood ... near Egersund," said Lars.

"How did you find it?"

"I just found it," said Lars.

"Lying on the ground?"

"Yes."

"When did you find it?"

"Not so long ago," he said, with a shrug.

"But when *exactly*?" I wanted a straight answer.

"I don't know. Before I left Norway," he replied.

"Well, that's obvious, isn't it! But *when*? A week before? A month? And *where* exactly? Did you find anything else?"

Lars said nothing. He just looked down.

What was wrong with him? I needed to ask more questions. What was Lars doing in this mysterious wood? Had he been alone? These questions and a thousand more crowded into my mind. But I'd hardly uttered a word when Lars stopped me, his voice loud and emphatic.

"I said I just found it!"

"You're hiding something." I wasn't going to let him fob me off.

Lars looked up, his face as pale as the snow. "Don't ask me any more, Jakob," his voice wobbled. "It was a wood near Egersund. Believe me, you don't want to know more."

The panic in his voice shocked me. Lars was nearly always completely calm. This was only the second time I'd seen him rattled. I knew if I pushed him any further there'd be no saying how he would react (after all, he'd smashed Sergeant Sneyd's dummy into bits). Now, up in the mountains with the night pressing in on us, I made one of the toughest decisions of my life. It wasn't the time or place to start questioning Lars. I would have to wait.

I took a long look at the little button compass and then turned my attention to reading the dial.

"South-south-east. We're on course," I said, pointing to a rise in the ground up ahead.

We set off again across the valley, making a straight furrow through the snow. The sky behind us was shot through with dark red and vivid pinks, but I barely noticed. I skied automatically, my mind circling round and round this business of the compass. I could think of nothing else. Had Father dropped it? What was he doing in a wood? His last mission was secret – he was never allowed to say where he was going or what he was doing. And why wouldn't Lars tell me anything more?

Just after sunset we reached the mountain range above the hut and stopped to get out our torches. I didn't know when I'd get another chance to talk to Lars on his own, so I tried once more.

"Lars, please—" I said, shining my torch towards his face.

But before I could stumble out another question, he said, "Jakob, you can keep that button."

And, without waiting for an answer, he pushed off on his ski poles and was gone.

Åse Jeffries

30TH DECEMBER 1942

Food at last!

Last night Jakob and Lars came home with a reindeer. I was so hungry I barely noticed that Lars was even more tense and unhappy than usual. All I saw was the blood down the front of his anorak.

Either he'd had a nosebleed, or…

Yes! Yes! YES! They'd shot a large reindeer.

We had the tongue for supper. I thought tongue would be just a tasty little morsel, but it's a huge wedge of

A tasty little mors

muscle that reaches far back into the throat. We also ate the cheeks, the palate, and the fat from behind the eyeballs. Delicious!

I'd been dreaming of steaks and fillets and chops, but now that we have all this meat it's the gristly, knobbly, slightly yeuchy bits that I really want to eat. Fred says this is because our bodies are crying out for fat, and the reindeers' cartilage, the organs and the fat are the most nutritious parts. He says the Sami people in Lapland throw the lean reindeer meat to their dogs.

Anyway, along with the meat we had our usual side dish of reindeer moss. But this moss was a bit different because it came from the dead reindeer's stomach and was already semi-digested. That didn't make for much of an improvement – there was a slight faecal aroma to it. Give me cod liver oil any day.

Afterwards we sat around the stove gnawing at knuckles of vertebra. Lars pulled out a long thin bit of leg sinew and used it as dental floss. Then I flung a slice of liver at Fred because he was getting on my nerves and he grabbed it off the floor and flung it back.

I think we're turning into cavemen.

Fred has been in radio contact with London again. We're due to attack on the night of the fourth of January. The heavy water stores will be collected from the plant on the sixth of January for shipping to Germany, so we have to get in before then. That gives us three more nights here before we move hut.

Åse Jeffries

This morning we had a huge breakfast of liver and brisket. Jakob and Lars have gone hunting again. Meanwhile Fred and I have done some housework and taken the meat outside and hung it in two sacks from the roof. Freddie's legs are beginning to look a bit more normal and he's no longer finding it hard to walk. He puts this down to eating all that moss.

The meat is frozen now, but the sacks have dripped buckets of blood, so there's a truly grisly area just by the window where we chop up bones. Here the snow is all red and the meat sacks have weird beards of red icicles. Anyone visiting the hut would think it was inhabited by a bunch of savage trolls. And we're certainly beginning to look a bit troll-like – I'm the only one who's used a hairbrush since we got here.

After lunch I went outside for a pee. I'd just finished when I saw what I thought was a beaver standing up on its hind legs on the brow of the hill.

It's really difficult to work out how big things are in the snow – in all that whiteness there's nothing to give you a proper sense of scale – but this beaver did look very substantial.

The next thing I knew, the beaver was down on all fours and coming towards the hut. And there was another peculiar thing: this beaver had a lolloping, loose-limbed walk, rather like a bear's.

When it was about 200 metres away, I gave a little yelp.

Heepers jeepers! It *was* a bear.

Don't run! I thought. *I know I mustn't run.* Bears can move at up to fifty kilometres an hour, so he'd catch me in seconds.

I stood completely still.

The bear came padding up to the meat cache, its nose close to the ground. It had tiny, beady eyes and a long snout.

The bear sniffed around the ground, licking the blood off the snow. Then it reared up on its back legs and reached up for the sacks of meat.

I couldn't stand there and wait to be eaten. Now was my moment.

Dead slowly I took a step towards the door of the hut.

That was a very, *very* stupid thing to do.

The bear's head swivelled. It had seen me! It dropped back on to four paws and ran for me.

About two metres in front of me, it reared up on to its back legs, gigantic and terrifying, like a full-sized billiard table upended and toppling towards me. Only this billiard table was really angry and it had humungous claws.

I had nothing to lose. Absolutely terrified, I tried the technique of Maximum Noise, Maximum Trouble: "Who do you think you are! Go away! GO AWAY!" I screamed, waving my arms in the air to make me seem bigger than I was.

For a second this did the trick. The bear stared at me with its blank little eyes. Bears have corrugated cardboard for brains, and this fellow certainly wasn't going to be solving quadratic equations with Fred.

Then what did I do? I know this sounds crazy but I thought a little surprise might put him off his guard. Why not show off before you get eaten? Might as well leave this world in style...

So I bent my legs and did a back flip.

It wasn't a perfect performance. The snow was too soft to get a good take off and somehow I under-rotated and landed *splat* on my stomach in the snow.

I looked up at the bear.

It blinked moronically, then bared its teeth. I remember thinking how pink its mouth was...

Then came the terrible moment: the bear lunged for me.

I heard a gun go off, but the bear was crashing

towards me. I ducked down, burying my head in my arms.

But the blow didn't come.

I crouched, shivering, my eyes barely open.

The bear lay crumpled in the snow in front of me.

And then who should appear, but Frederick Haukerd. He was carrying a gun.

"Hmm," said Fred, leaning over the bear. "I got it in the stomach. He took ages to drop, didn't he? Must be the slow metabolic rate. A bear's heart only beats once every four seconds. Very odd to find one round here. Not really their neck of the woods. Should be further north. Perhaps this is a particularly bad winter."

Did Fred then add, "Are you OK, Åse?" or "That must have been a nasty shock – have a cup of tea." Of course not.

Instead, he took a small measuring tape from his pocket. "I've never had an opportunity to get this close," he enthused. "Look at this! The claw's eleven centimetres long. Now Åse, if he'd got your carotid artery you'd be—"

"Thanks, Fred!" I interrupted. "No doubt you're delighted I haven't died of shock." It sounded a bit thin given that he'd just saved my life. So I added, "By the way, I think your Marmite jar's in one of the explosive bags."

UNUSUAL FACTS ABOUT BEARS
BY FREDERICK HAUKERD

1. Bears are surprisingly noisy. They bark and make popping noises with their jaws. Suckling cubs make a sound a little like humming.

2. Brown and black bears can <u>DOUBLE</u> their weight between the spring and the autumn.

3. Unlike sheep, no two bears look the same – you can always tell them apart because of their distinctive faces and fur markings.

4. Bears tread in each other's footsteps. Where a bear has left tracks in the ground, another bear coming later will tread in exactly the same places. In soft ground this means that bear tracks can be as deep as twenty-five centimetres. No one knows the reason for this curious behaviour.

5. Black bears aren't always black. They can be cinnamon coloured or even white (sometimes called "spirit bears").

6. Towards autumn, bears become "hyperphagic" – their bodies crave food and they are obsessed with eating. At this time of year a brown bear will eat 15,000 calories in a day – six or seven times what an adult man normally eats.

7. Bears are not fussy eaters. They will consume entire anthills, eating the earth along with the insects.

8. Bears sometimes "bluff charge". This means that they come racing towards their victim and then stop or veer off at the last moment.

9. Nobody understands how bears survive hibernation. When large mammals sleep for a long time, they normally build up uric acid in the muscles which in turn damages the internal organs. Bears can cope with months of sleep without this happening.

BROWN BEAR

Fred looked pleased. "Splendid! Now, will you help me measure its skull? Then we can examine the contents of its stomach."

I made a dash for the hut.

Tonight Jakob and Lars came back with two more deer. I never thought I would say this, but I think we have *too much food*.

Åse Jeffries

The carcasses are coming in handy in all sorts of ways. We've put the skins down on the floor (the bear is nice and thick, but *very* smelly). And, as the window keeps frosting over, I've made a little lamp by chewing up reindeer fat (Lars's tip – it makes the fat easier to burn) and using a piece of string as the wick. Freddie has turned the bear's bladder into a balloon for his new baby brother. He says the bladder would also make a wonderful flotation device and that if I get attacked by a second bear (perish the thought!) he'll make a pair of bellows for the stove. He also muttered something about constructing a bagpipe.

In fact the sky's the limit when you're as bored as we are. If we stay here much longer I think we'll be making model boats out of the bone chippings.

Fred's legs are fine now – the swelling has gone. And there's been a lot of communication with London, normally late at night. We've been told the Germans are getting edgy, so they must be getting ready to ship the heavy water. They've replaced the Austrian guards at Vemork with crack German troops and altered the times of the sentry changes. The garrison at the Mosvatn dam (about fifteen kilometres away) has been increased and anti-aircraft guns and searchlights have been set up. There's also a signals tracking station – so they must suspect there's a secret transmitter somewhere around – but they haven't searched the mountains yet. Having spent more than three weeks up here, I can see why.

London has told Fred that the commander at Vemork is off to Oslo on Thursday for a long weekend, so the crack guards might be a bit less cracking and a bit more beer-filled than usual.

We now have three days before the attack and tomorrow we leave the hut. It seems unimaginable. It feels as though we've been here since the dawn of time. Our world has shrunk to the size of these few floorboards. I now know every seam in the floor here and I can tell you what's on page 32 of the August 1942 edition of *Angling Times*. That's hardly going to help me face crack German troops...

Jakob P. Stromsheim

2ND JANUARY 1943

A clear, cold day and we've done the hut move – eight kilometres, mostly downhill and through crisp snow, taking the toboggan and some chunks of bear and reindeer meat with us. Our new residence is not a bad hut, but it's at Fjosbudalen, only five kilometres from Rjukan. We're on a very steep slope, on the opposite side of the valley from the Vemork plant, and we are no longer safely tucked away up in the wild plateau, so the Germans are more likely to find us. Now we have to be really careful. One of us is on watch all the time and we've blacked out the windows with bits of old blanket.

This evening we sat down with the plans and aerial photographs. The Vemork power plant is like a fortress. It's on a shelf of rock, dug into the mountainside in a very dark and precipitous valley. Below the plant the cliff face is vertical. If one of the guards dropped a cigarette butt over the edge of the mountain it would fall 200 metres straight down into the River Mane at the bottom.

So we have a choice:

1. We can approach the plant from above, where the slope is more manageable. But the Germans must be expecting an attack from here because they've mined the mountainside and set up machine-gun batteries and booby traps, as well as every sort of tripwire you could imagine. The odds aren't good either: four of us against thirty troops!

2. We can approach via the suspension bridge that crosses the gorge and leads to the road through the valley. But this is maximum visibility and we're certain to get gunned down by the two Germans who patrol the bridge.

So that only leaves us with what Åse calls the "impossible option".

3. We sneak in from below, cross the deep, fast-

flowing river at the bottom of the gorge and climb a completely vertical cliff. The only good thing going for this plan is that the Germans, who must believe that nobody would be so foolish as to try this route, don't seem to have paid much attention to defending the cliff.

I've asked Lars to go and have a look at the gorge tomorrow and see if he can chart a route for us. In the meantime there's nothing much we can do except rest and try not to panic!

Åse Jeffries

3RD JANUARY 1943

Lars was back by lunchtime, glowering slightly less than normal. He thinks the cliff is doable – *just*.

The ice on the river at the bottom of the gorge is breaking up, but there's still one point where we can get across. Lars did it twice today and he thinks the ice will hold until tomorrow night, especially if the weather stays cold.

As for the ascent, Lars has found a place a few hundred metres downstream from the suspension bridge where there are some small trees and shrubs growing up the cliff face.

"I thought that if trees could grow in that gorge,

then we could climb it," he said. "I had a go and it wasn't easy, but there were enough toeholds to keep me going."

"Well, that's pretty good news," I said. "But firstly you weren't carrying a pack of explosives on your back, secondly you weren't climbing at night, and thirdly I'm about half your size, so how am I supposed to get up that cliff?"

Lars grimaced slightly. "You'll probably make it," he said.

Huh!

"Well, that's sorted," said Jakob, who didn't seem worried that I might *not* make it. "But what about the escape? Should we try and creep back down the cliff face? Or should we just take the quickest route and shoot our way out across the suspension bridge? The odds are heavily against us…"

In the end, Jakob decided that we should try to go back down the cliff, unless we were already in a shoot-out. It seems less brave, but being sneaky and small and unexpected are our best weapons. (There are, very occasionally, moments in life when I have to agree with Colonel Armstrong.)

Once the attack is over we'll divide into pairs and make our way to Sweden. If we ever get that far…

For supper Jakob and I cooked a fantastic stew (Fred

was busy telegramming London) with some dried peas (thank you, Fjosbudalen hut) and a huge amount of reindeer. I can't understand why we've let Fred do all the cooking up till now, when there's always the danger that he'll experiment with some new bizarre flavouring. But when I said this to Jakob, he just winked at me. He's too tactful to get drawn into arguments.

We've gone off the bear meat a bit. It's *very* strong – like ten-year-old mutton. Maybe getting faddy is a sign that we're not so desperately hungry as we were. A week ago I would have eaten anything!

Åse Jeffries

4TH JANUARY 1943

Tonight WE LEAVE FOR THE RAID! We've waxed our skis and packed and rechecked our bags. Pickaxes, ropes, knives, explosives and the last of the chocolate, specially saved for tonight. In our trouser pockets we've each got a little gauze pad and a glass phial of chloroform so that we can knock out a guard completely silently. Then there are always the cyanide capsules… (We keep them in different places. I've sewn mine into my coat pocket, and Lars has his in the cuff of his shirt. Jakob and Fred have these special, tiny inner pockets in their trousers.)

We've tried to think of everything. We've even chosen passwords in case we should get split up in the dark and need to confirm who someone is. The question is "Leicester Square?" The answer: "Piccadilly".

But let's get back to the one thing I'm trying not to think about: the *raid*. After lunch Jakob said he needed to talk to everybody. He was looking really pale and I knew he was going to say something important.

He took a breath and started. "If we are caught tonight we'll certainly be killed. And before we're killed, we'll be tortured. We don't know what they'll do – but that interrogation at Drumincraig will be nothing compared with what could come our way. Lars, I'm sure you can put up with a lot of pain—" Lars looked at the ground and said nothing "—but however brave we are, none of us can be sure that we won't cave in and talk. So I think we owe it to each other, to our families, to Norway and to all the Allies to take our own lives before that happens. If you are captured and can't get away you must put that pill in your mouth and bite hard. Remember to bite it. Swallowing is not good enough – the rubber on the capsule is very thick and it could pass straight through you."

He paused. "I want you all to promise."

And just then I had what I thought was a humdinger of an idea. "Let's swear on this," I said, and I brought out of my bag a little Victorian dolls' house Bible that has been with me through my worst times at Roxbury Hall and which I sneaked into my rucksack at Drumincraig. The book is tiny – only about the length of my little finger, and the paper is so thin and the print so small you can only just read it. But it's still a Bible.

I held it in the palm of my hand and said, "I hereby swear by Almighty God that under no circumstance will I let myself be taken alive."

After me, Lars took the Bible and swore on it too.

But Fred, who is never straightforward and never makes anything easy, promptly declared that he was an atheist.

"The Bible does not constitute verifiable fact," he said. "I'm not swearing on anything I don't believe in."

"All right, Freddie," said Jakob, for ever the peace-maker. "Is there anything in your bag you *would* be willing to swear on?"

Fred thought for a minute, then rummaged around

in his rucksack. I thought he was going to produce his Marmite jar – which is definitely verifiable fact – but instead he brought out the rather pungent bear's bladder balloon that he'd made for his baby brother. He made his pledge on that.

The last to take his oath was Jakob. He took out the little button compass from his pocket and placed it upright in his palm. As he did so, he and Lars exchanged what you might call a Look. Since I read Jakob's entries in the log I've been really curious about the compass and wanted to have a good snoop at it. But the atmosphere was very tense and Jakob looked like he didn't want to be asked any questions at all. So, just for once, I restrained myself and kept quiet. I deserve a medal!

Åse Jeffries

As we're going to be up all night it seemed sensible to lie down and get some rest. We've spent the afternoon in our sleeping bags by the fire, but nobody has slept a wink. I tried to, but I was in such a state of nerves that at times I could hear my heart thumping away as if it were a rat trying to break out of my ribcage.

It's six thirty now. It's dark outside and Fred is cooking supper. We're to set off at eight o'clock so that we get to Vemork just before the midnight sentry change. Our preparations are done. Now it's a matter of waiting, and that's probably the worst bit of all.

This will probably be my last entry. I know we're unlikely to succeed, and escaping afterwards will be all but impossible.

I'm signing off now – I need some time to write a letter to my family. I'm glad we've kept this log – it may give those who come looking for us some idea of what we've been through.

Dear Mum and Pop,

I want you to know that I love you both VERY MUCH and give Trudie a big hug too. I know I haven't been a perfect daughter, but I have tried my best. So please forgive me for the times when I've disobeyed you, or been crabby and annoying.

Mum, give my gymnastics cups to Trudie, who I adore (even if she is perfect...). Of course I want you to remember me but please don't keep my bedroom frozen in time, with all the books and things perfectly arranged like in some creepy museum. Let Tru move in. She's always wanted the bigger room.

Celebrate my birthday every year with a gigantic chocolate cake. And give Max a doggie treat and a final tummy scratch from me.

If you do find my body please let me lie by Grandpa and Grandma in that little graveyard in Skudneshaven where there's nothing but sea and sky and wind. It is so perfect. Sorry for this rather shaky hand.

Your ever loving daughter,

Åse

Jakob P. Stromsheim

5TH JANUARY 1943

We've made it to Vemork! We're resting in the old electrical converter hut outside the plant until the guard changes. Then we'll have to go in. This is what's happened so far.

At eight o'clock we were standing in the dark outside the hut with the wind whipping the snow up round our legs. This was it. For a moment I wished I was back home with Mother. Help! It was so cold and so frightening, and everything rested on the next few hours. Then a stern little voice inside me said, "Get a grip, boy! Remember your duty!"

So I braced myself, leaned forward on my ski poles and looked at everyone carefully in turn. I had to know for sure that no one had had a change of heart. Lars, Freddie and Åse all had their balaclavas down with only their eyes showing through the slits. It was a bit like looking at people through a postbox. But they nodded back at me.

"All right," I said, trying to make my voice sound firm. "Let's go."

Lars led the way. The slope headed steeply downhill and, as I was the last to go, it was as if my friends were

181

simply disappearing over the edge of the mountain. I set off after them and I soon realized that this really was a wonderful ski run. The piste was as long and as straight as a playground chute.

After a while, we came to the treeline where the land was broken up with odd stumps and bits of brush. We took off our skis, put them on our shoulders and started to climb downwards. The going was hard – great spiky juniper bushes blocked the way and the snow had collected in huge drifts, sometimes over a metre high. The mountainside was still very steep and often we were half tumbling, half sliding downwards, with only the tree trunks to break our fall. Åse calls this "skambling" – part skiing, part falling, part tumbling.

Eventually we reached the road through the valley. Here we brushed ourselves down, put our skis back on and glided down the road, keeping to the edges where the snow was still soft.

We followed the road as it twisted its way down the valley. We were much more exposed now and I pulled back my balaclava so I'd be able to hear any approaching cars. But I could hear only a slight, dull hum in the air, like the sound of a city in the far distance, which grew louder as we descended.

Finally we turned a corner and – at last! – on the

far side of the gorge, I saw the power station. It was all lit up in the moonlight – as huge and forbidding as a Transylvanian castle, with the deep gorge in front acting as a moat. The hum was now clearly separate sounds – water rushing through the sluices, the whirl of dynamos and a more general clatter of machinery.

Freddie stood beside me, his goggles dangling off his chin. He looked completely transfixed. "Crikey!" he said. "It's a whopper! They used 1,700 barrels of cement and 800 tonnes of steel just to build the main electrolysis building. There's 50 cubic metres of water going through those penstocks every second—"

"Come on." I tugged at his sleeve. "This isn't the time. We've got to get off the road."

And, at the very moment I said this, headlights swerved round the corner only ten metres in front of us.

"Geddown!" I shouted. Fear made me very fast. I pulled Freddie down with me into the ditch at the side of the road and there we crouched, skis and sticks tangled together. Slowly – *so* very slowly – the beams of the headlights passed over the top of our ditch and the vehicle trundled on up the hill. It was a miracle they hadn't see us. I was shocked – it had been a close call.

But Freddie seemed completely unfazed.

"That must be the bus for the workers on the night

183

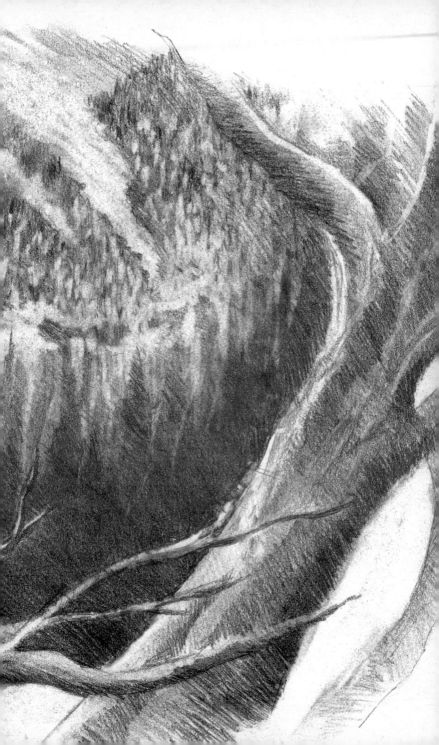

shift," he whispered, sticking his head out over the top of the ditch.

"Stay down!" I yanked him back just as another set of headlights scanned the road. A second large, heavy vehicle passed by.

"Now I remember," grinned Freddie. "There are two buses for the night shift, aren't there?"

I managed not to say anything.

Back on the road Åse and Lars emerged from behind a large mound of snow. After the near miss, everything we were doing felt so much more scary and real – the headlights had been a sort of awakening. I felt jumpier than before.

We skied on until we reached an old power line road which branched off up the mountain to the east. Lars led us 50 metres along the road and then we veered off into a dark wood. In a small clearing we took off our skis.

It was a sheltered spot, but I could still feel the wind on my cheeks. It came in little gusts and was strangely warm – warmer and drier than the air around me. Bad news. It was a *foehn*, a high-pressure wind coming down from the mountains, getting warmer and warmer as it descended. The last thing we wanted was a *foehn* – the warm air melts the snow and ice. If the ice on the River Mane melted, we wouldn't be able to cross the river and the whole mission would be lost. We couldn't swim that river and survive – not even Lars could do it.

I put my balaclava back on and pressed my fingers against my jacket so I could feel the little button compass in my pocket. There was absolutely nothing to be done.

We hid the skis under a pile of snowy spruce branches, then we checked our guns and pistols and Lars and I put on the special packs holding the explosives. Freddie took the metal shears and Lars looped a long coil of rope around his middle.

Lastly we shared out the hand grenades and the extra ammunition. Åse stowed away the very last of the chocolate in her pocket.

It was now ten o'clock. In two and a half hours we'd be inside the plant.

There was no going back.

I nodded to Lars and we set off down the mountainside.

At the bottom of the gorge my worst fears came true. The *foehn* had done its work; the ice on the river was gone. Lars and I looked at each other and shook our heads. Why was *everything* so difficult?

We made our way along the bank with Lars in the lead. The river, fed by melt water in the mountains, roared past us in full spate. A hundred metres further down, we came to a bend in the river, overshadowed by dripping birch trees. Here Lars stopped and pointed to a large rock beside the river.

"This is where I crossed," he shouted over the roar of the river.

I looked at him in disbelief. He couldn't be serious!

There was *some* ice there. But it was no flat ice bridge – just a few semi-submerged lumps bobbing up and down in the rushing water. Only one large island of ice remained near the far bank.

We climbed to the edge of the river bank.

"I'm light. I'll go first," said Åse. And before any of us could protest, she jumped onto the first block of ice. It rocked under her, and she wobbled a bit and had to stretch out her arms to gain her balance. She stepped onto the next piece of ice. "Whoa." She steadied herself. Then, nimble as a hare, she hopped onto the next block. And the next. And the next. There was a large gap before the big ice island. She jumped this, righted herself and stepped onto the bank on the far side, giving us a thumbs-up.

Freddie had been surveying Åse's progress gloomily. "That's all very well," he said. "But she's light as a flea *and* she's a champion gymnast."

I put my arm round him. "I know. I thought she'd fit in a cartwheel. But cheer up, Freddie. It's not so bad."

Lars went next. He took a slightly different route, only using the bigger blocks of ice, but jumping further between each one.

When he reached the far bank, Freddie turned to me. "You go next," he said.

"Not on your life!" I said. "My job is to bring up the rear. Come on, Freddie. You'll make it. Think of it as a rather difficult book where every lump of ice is a different chapter."

Freddie was not *at all* convinced. But, very gingerly, he stepped onto the first ice block, where he lurched horribly to and fro with his arms flapping in the air. I couldn't bear to watch, so I just stared at the ground, held my breath and waited. Thankfully he managed to right himself.

"This is *not* fun!" he exclaimed.

"Keep going. Use your momentum."

Freddie moved on to the next ice block and executed another very wobbly landing. But after that he seemed to get the hang of it and made his way across the river quite smoothly.

I followed him over and, as I reached the far bank, I looked up at the side of the gorge we now had to climb.

The cliff was a huge, vertical slab of rock about 200 metres high – that's the height of ten or twelve Drumincraig Houses piled one on top of another. In the

darkness, I couldn't see the summit, but I could sense that it was very, very far away. This climb would go on and on and on. In fact the cliff face might as well continue up into the stratosphere – we'd never get to the top.

What made matters worse was the surface of the rock. It was as if it had been sliced out of the mountainside with a gigantic and very sharp blade. Lars was right when he said there were trees and shrubs growing on the rock. But the plants were only present in some places and, even then, they seemed to emerge from the tiniest cracks and crevices. Otherwise the cliff face was sheer.

How could we climb this? I looked down at the ground. The bed of the gorge was solid rock and ice. If we fell, we would die.

I took off my gloves and put the palm of my hand against the cliff face. The stone was wet and slimy, with melt water pouring down in tiny rivulets. I'd never dreaded something so much in my life.

Åse also leaned a bare hand against the stone. "Yeuch." She wiped her hand on her camouflage suit. "It'll be like climbing a blancmange. We'll be slipping all the time."

She was dead right. But it was my job to try and sound encouraging. "Look, the sooner we get started the better," I said. "These things are never so bad once you're doing them. Just don't look down."

I waited until Freddie and Åse had got some way up the cliff face before I started the climb.

For the first 50 metres, everything went well. Even if I did have to stretch a lot, my hands and feet were always able to grope their way to some little crevice or outcrop in the rock and clutch on to it. Sometimes these holds were just tiny cracks and sometimes they were so nearly out of my reach that I had to rely on them before I was really sure that they'd hold my weight. I just kept on going up: right hand, left hand, right foot, left foot…

I couldn't see much – the moonlight didn't seem to get down into this part of the gorge – and I felt very alone, clinging to the sheer cliff with nothing to keep me company but the far off drone of the power station and the *swoosh* of melt water running down the crevices.

After a while, my fingers began to ache. Then one of my legs got the shakes. I stopped, shut my eyes, concentrated on my breathing and waited.

The spasm in my leg ended and I opened my eyes again. I slid my right hand across the rock face, feeling for a hold.

There was nothing there.

I stretched my hand out further. Even a tiny crevice would do… There was nothing.

I carefully switched hands and tried with my left hand, reaching up and down and back and forth. The rock face was smooth as glass, but with outstretched fingers I could just feel the tips of a plant hanging down the cliff.

I peered through the darkness – the plant was some sort of long, hanging shrub. Stretching as far as I possibly could, I swung my body back and forth, but the shrub was still too far away. I stopped. I *had* to stay calm. I waited a moment, then reached out again. Still my fingers were clutching at air.

I was breathing hard now, and I didn't know if this was from panic or exhaustion.

What did I do now?

I looked down.

It was the stupidest thing I could have done. There was just darkness and far, far below a tiny winding string of silver, which was, of course, the river. One wrong move, one twitch of a muscle, and I would fall to my death.

There was only one thing I could do and I had to do it now, before my fingers went numb.

In one final, desperate leap, I swung my body out across the cliff face and at the last moment I let go of the ledge and reached for the shrub.

For a fraction of a second I was in mid-air holding on to nothing. Then my hand – thank goodness – closed around the plant and somehow it took my weight. Gasping for breath, I pulled myself up. I could hear the roots of the shrub tearing, but I'd found a foothold and I hoisted myself up until I was able to get hold of the ledge that the shrub was growing out of. There was also a small pine tree there and I'd just got my arm round the trunk when a gust of wind roared along the rock face and pulled hard at my back. I clung to the trunk.

Slowly the wind eased off and at last I could breathe again.

I knew then that I must have a guardian angel.

I set off once more on the climb. My nerves were better now that I'd chanced all and won. Soon I was back to my old rhythm: right hand, left hand, right foot, left foot... But I couldn't shake the thought that if the wind had come a minute earlier, I would've been a mangled heap at the bottom of the gorge.

When I finally scrambled over the top of the cliff onto the ledge, I discovered that Lars and Åse were already at the top. But Freddie was still some way down the cliff. I must have overtaken him at some point. If I'd found that climb hard, how on earth was Freddie getting on?

Lars and I took the climbing rope, tied it to a larch tree and dropped the end over the edge near to Freddie. It only went down a short way, but at least it reached him.

After that, I lay down flat on my stomach with my face over the edge of the cliff and whispered encouraging things to Freddie.

At last, he was near enough to reach my hand and I leaned over, grabbed him under the arms and hauled him up onto the ledge. He lay there for a minute, pale and shaky and out of breath.

"It'll be easier when we go back," I said. "We can belay down the rope for the first part."

Freddie nodded. He flexed his hand. "My metacarpi are stiff."

"Your what?"

"My fingers," said Freddie. "They're stiff. And my toes. I need a little chocolate. Medicinal purposes. I have to soften the ligaments. Otherwise I might have problems using those bolt cutters."

"What garbage!" snorted Åse. "You're not going to be playing a piano sonata. You're only opening a gate."

All the same, she delved into her pocket, brought out a block of chocolate and broke off eight squares.

"Let's all have some," she said.

The chocolate did cheer us up. We took off our packs and ate it really slowly – as if it were our very last meal. And it was *so* delicious!

We were still about a kilometre away from the plant, but the two huge pale buildings of Vemork stood out against the mountainside.

The ledge we were sitting on was about three metres wide and skirted the side of the mountain. Along its length ran a small railway track that carried trolleys of coal from Rjukan village up to the power station. All we had to do now was follow this track. But there remained one big problem: mines.

This smooth, level path was just too good to be true. Surely the Germans would have laid tripwires and mines in the area all around, just as they'd done on the slopes above the power station? And, of course, there was only one way to find out... We had to test the ground.

"I'll go ahead," said Lars.

I looked at him, sitting there all stony-faced. I didn't know quite what Lars's demons were, but I was sure he didn't expect to come back from this mission. In fact I suspected he was *hoping* not to survive.

"Thanks, Lars," I said, because it was still a very brave offer on his part. "But I'm doing this bit. You can't be spared. Nobody else really knows their way round the Hardanger like you do. This part is my job." And I gave him a look that said, *This isn't up for discussion.*

I handed Åse the rucksack with the explosives, then I set off down the track. Although I was trying not to show how scared I was, at first I walked very carefully and lightly. But after a while I realized this was slowing me up too much and I had to walk more normally. If a mine was to blow my head off it'd do so anyway, whether I was on tiptoe or not.

So I walked on in the moonlight, with the hum of the plant buzzing in my head. The wind was rising, pulling the snow from the boughs of the fir trees. Everything felt a little unreal – as if I was watching myself from afar. I wondered what I should be thinking about, when every step might be my last and I decided to rest my mind on good things: an Errol Flynn film I saw on my last birthday at home, Mother's scones, games of tennis in the summer, a fishing trip in Lake Tarlebøvatnet with Father. But that, of course, brought me back to the mystery of the little button compass and how it had ended up with Lars.

When I'd walked a hundred paces I turned and beckoned the others on. They were to follow, always keeping some distance behind and walking in my footprints.

I continued on down the track. After a short while I came to some footprints in the snow. These were old prints – the snow had crumbled and thawed around them – and they put my mind at rest. If the staff at the power plant were walking down by the railway line the ground *must* be safe.

I followed the footsteps and, round a bend in the trees, I came to the small shed we'd spotted on the plans. At last!

I opened the door on an enormous electrical converter.

And this is where I'm writing. There's plenty of room inside and it's warm and dry and out of the wind. The others have arrived too and we're hunkered down at the back of the hut, where there's a small window looking out over the suspension bridge. Outside I can see a scattering of lights from the village of Vaer on the far side of the gorge. How far we've come!

Åse Jeffries

5TH JANUARY 1943

By the time we got to the hut I was bushwhacked. All that clinging on to rock faces had done something very strange to the muscles in my hands and my fingers felt as if they'd been chopped off and put back on again the wrong way round. As for my legs, I could barely feel them at all. But hey! I was still alive.

It was nearly midnight and for some time everyone had been very quiet, wrapped up in their own thoughts, apart from Jakob, who was scribbling away in the log. It was a good, companionable silence (although there *was* something rather scary about the way Fred fiddled with his mini flask of chloroform). Anyway, I felt so close to all of the boys. I realized that even Lars, who was sitting by my side chewing a matchstick and staring out the window, no longer seemed like an alien to me.

Suddenly Lars pointed to the barracks. Two men were coming out carrying rifles.

The enemy! Real German soldiers! The first I'd ever seen! And of course they didn't look anything like the terrible cartoons of the Hun. They were just like you or me.

The men walked slowly down the hill, towards the suspension bridge. One of them was a tall, skinny beanpole of a man and the other was squat and sort of blob-shaped. They weren't exactly hurrying – I've seen coffin-bearers move faster – but then nobody would be exactly rushing off to spend a night standing on a suspension bridge in a high wind.

The tall German was waving his arms about, and the squat one seemed to be nodding.

They stopped. The tall one was explaining something that needed two hands. He was holding his arms out as if to show the size of something. What was it? A fish he'd caught on holiday?

These soldiers had no idea what tonight had in store for them. They couldn't know that they were about to play a role in history. Their jobs and possibly their lives (I don't think Hitler really suffers bunglers) were on the line. And the future of Europe, and of the world, hung in the balance.

And what were they doing? Discussing a fishing trip!

In five minutes we were to go in. Then it'd all be up to me and I'd be squeezing my way between high-voltage electric cables so tight that I wouldn't be able to turn round or probably even breathe.

What if I got stuck? I tried hard not to think of my pet frog Humboldt. Last summer I brought poor Humboldt into the house for a little swim in our bath. Being an idiot, I let the plug out while Humboldt was still frolicking on a sponge. Quick as quick he jumped into the downpipe and promptly got himself stuck. And there he stayed, croaking pathetically, until Dad put him out of his misery with a chisel.

Nothing worse than poor Humboldt's fate could befall me. I just hoped that there was enough room in the chute for me to reach for my white capsule.

It was time to check my charges and say a quick prayer.

Jakob P. Stromsheim

5TH JANUARY 1943

At precisely midnight, we left the hut and made our way towards the plant. We crouched down among the trees beside the gate. Up close, the power plant was a truly terrifying prospect. Everything seemed so big.

The great electrolysis building where they stored the

heavy water was a monstrous hulk of steel and glass, with machinery rumbling angrily somewhere in its bowels. Behind it loomed the great metal pipes of the penstocks (sluices that control the water flow). Even the gate – four metres tall and padlocked shut with a chain as thick as your arm – was not to be trifled with.

I felt very small and very scared, but we had to go on. We had to go in.

The guards' barracks, a long rectangular building on the far side of the gate, lay about thirty paces away – well within shooting range. I took the safety catch off my Tommy gun and pointed the muzzle at the ground.

Then I glanced at Freddie. His job was to run ahead and break open the gate. He looked keen – in fact, he looked a little too keen.

"Try and do it quietly," I whispered. "We don't want to wake the soldiers, OK?"

"Don't worry," he said happily. "They'll be used to odd noises. They'll have small hydrogen explosions here all the time."

Freddie ran to the gate. He positioned the shears round the chain and, as he gave a great wrench to the chain, I screwed up my eyes and cringed in anticipation.

A screech of tearing metal rang out in the night air. Then came a deafening jangle as Freddie let the broken chain clang against the gate.

The noise would've woken the dead. And that's what was so peculiar. I looked in all directions. Nothing happened. No siren, no floodlights, no sound came from the barracks, and no guards appeared.

Could we really be so lucky?

By now Freddie was through the gate and running along the inside edge of the fence. He came to a second gate, which he broke open to give us another way out of the complex if we got trapped. Again the sound was incredibly loud, but again, there was no reaction from the barracks. Maybe Freddie was right and the guards really *were* used to bangs and clangs in the night.

I crept through the first gate, dashed to the back wall of the barracks and crouched down low. Here Freddie joined me. I listened, but the noise of the machinery was just the same as before. All was clear. I beckoned to Lars and Åse, who were still out among the trees. Lars ran through the gate and took up position behind a storage tank. Åse followed, stopping to close the gate and wrap the chain back around the handle.

I edged my way along the wall of the barracks and stuck my head round the corner. Between the barracks and the electrolysis building lay a large open courtyard speckled with strange little dots of light, like thousands of tiny eyes. I couldn't work this out. I looked up at the building and then suddenly I understood: the windows had been blacked out with paint, but the job had been crudely done, leaving cracks between the brushstrokes. Hence the little lights everywhere.

We had to cross this open courtyard. I put my forefinger on the trigger of the Tommy gun and felt for the pistol in my holster. There was complete silence from the barracks – the guards must have been sleeping. Up on the mountainside I could see the guard stationed at the penstocks, but he had his back to the plant.

It was time to go. Lars and Åse were still crouched by the storage tank. I gave them the thumbs up.

Lars raced across the courtyard and disappeared round the corner of the building. Then Åse followed. Freddie went next and I was the last to run across.

On this side the plant was less exposed. There were no barracks here, and the snowdrifts at the edge of the building provided some cover, but my heart was still pounding.

We crept along the wall and came to the heavy metal door that led down to the basement. Lars tried the handle, but the door was bolted, just as we'd expected.

We carried on till we came to a ground floor window, which was poorly blacked out. I found a keyhole sized gap in the paint and peered in.

Phew! We *were* in the right place. Down below me was a basement room with two rows of large, gleaming metal drums. I knew this room very, very well. It looked just like its replica back at Drumincraig. The metal drums – eighteen of them – contained the heavy water cells. This was our target.

But something *was* different. The room now had a new, human component! In between the two rows of drums was a man sitting at a table, with his back to the window. The man looked old, with thinning hair and a stooped back. If his shabby overalls were anything to go by, he was a civilian. So he would be a Norwegian.

Åse elbowed me in the ribs and pointed further along the building to a metal flap set high up on the wall.

"The electrical duct," she whispered.

The flap was a couple of metres off the ground. Freddie cupped his hands and Åse clambered up until she was standing on Lars's shoulders. (We'd practised this manoeuvre a zillion times.) Åse tried the flap, but it didn't move. Swaying slightly, she took out a small metal pick from her jacket pocket and inserted it into the lock at the bottom of the flap. She moved the pick carefully up and down until the lock gave. Then she lifted up the flap. The hole looked horribly small.

She turned back to me.

"Wish me luck!" she whispered. Then, ever so nimbly, she hoisted herself on to the lip of the tunnel and soon the flap closed behind her.

We waited. I felt dreadful – this was worse than anything else so far. For now we had nothing to distract us. All we could do was stand around and wait. And, of course, the longer we did so, the more likely it was that one of the guards would find us.

A minute later the flap reopened. Åse came out legs first and Lars guided her feet back on to his shoulders.

"What's the matter?" I asked.

"No use. It's been blocked off." Åse jumped down and wiped the dust off her shoulders. "It only goes back a few metres. Somebody's made a mistake."

"We'll have to break our way in," said Lars, striding over to the nearest window.

"No! Wait!" I hissed. Lars stopped.

I turned to Freddie. "Is there any other way in?" I asked.

We'd studied the plans of the power station in detail, but only Freddie would remember absolutely everything.

"Quick, Freddie! *Think*."

Freddie stared blankly at the night sky for what seemed an unbearably long time. Lars rocked on the balls of his feet and looked so impatient that I was afraid he'd just go ahead and break the window anyway. But then, *finally*, something came to Freddie.

"There's a second entrance that leads into the next room in the basement," he said. "Nobody seems sure about it – it's just a dotted line on the plans, but we've nothing to lose."

Freddie scanned the side of the building. "If it exists, it's in there," he said, pointing to a huge pile of snow banked up against the wall. "It'll be on this side," he added, "about a metre off the ground."

We dug away at the side of the snowdrift with our hands, pushing the snow out of the way until it formed another big mound behind us. We worked fast, but time was against us – a guard could appear any minute.

Suddenly Lars cried "Down!", and we ducked behind the mound of snow just as an open-backed jeep sped round the corner.

The jeep stopped about four metres away from us. I heard the door open, and then came the sound of German voices. I felt for the little capsule in the inner pocket of my trousers. I could feel panic rising. I looked over at Åse, who was listening to the men, following what they said. Her face looked pinched.

Then the door of the jeep slammed shut and the engine started up again. They drove past our mound and on round the plant.

Åse let out a sigh of relief.

"What was it?" I asked.

"They've noticed our footprints, but they think we're some of the Norwegian staff coming outside for an illegal cigarette break. We have to move fast. They're coming back."

"When?"

"You won't believe this! One of them has found a hole in the sole of his boots and doesn't fancy getting his feet wet. So they're going to stop off at the barracks for a change of boots and then they'll be back."

"That gives us about five minutes."

"If that!" said Lars.

We dug like maniacs, flinging snow in every direction. And then, thank goodness! My fingers found a small, square metal door about a metre off the ground. Åse released the lock with a flick of her metal pick and we opened up the flap.

The shaft was even narrower than the electrical duct and it stank of mice.

Åse grimaced. "An eel would find that tight."

"You'll be fine," I said breezily (I couldn't let her know how nervous I felt). "Just hunch your shoulders together and keep your nerve."

She clambered headfirst into the tunnel. "It's full of cobwebs," she whimpered.

"That means air must be circulating and they haven't blocked off the openings," said Freddie, as I held the flap open so she could see where she was going.

But she was hardly half a metre inside the tunnel when she stopped and let out a little yelp.

"I'm stuck!" she cried.

I reached in and gave her bottom a quick shove, but nothing happened. We had no time now. Those guards would be back any minute.

"Lars!" I cried. "Help!"

Lars gave a great heave and shoved with all his might.

There was another yelp and then Åse was free! She crawled away down the tunnel.

We crept back along the wall to the metal door and waited for her, guns at the ready. We were completely exposed. I looked at my watch. Four long minutes had passed – the guards would surely be getting back into the jeep.

We heard the bolt on the door being drawn back.

"Leicester Square?" asked a familiar voice.

"It's us, let us in!" I hissed.

"Leicester Square?" Åse asked again. I could've brained her! Above the roar of the machinery I could hear an engine starting up round the corner.

"Shut up, Åse! Let us in!"

"Why have passwords if we're not going to use them? Leicester Square?" she asked for a third time in her most hoity-toity voice.

I wanted to slap her. This wasn't a game! But my mind had gone completely blank. What was the password?

"Piccadilly," said Freddie.

The door opened.

We stormed through it as if we were being chased by wolves. I closed the door and, as I did so, I heard the patrol jeep drive round the corner of the building. We'd only just made it.

Lars was about to fix back the heavy metal bolt but I grabbed his arm and shook my head. It was too late to lock the door. The jeep had stopped just outside and the guards were getting out. If we pulled the bolt now they'd hear us.

The guards were walking towards the door.

We had to hide.

I looked round, trying not to panic. We were in a windowless corridor with a metal spiral staircase leading to the floors above. On our right was the door to the room with the heavy water cells and the old man sitting at the desk. But at the far end of the corridor I spotted two large chest freezers and a row of lockers.

We ran along the corridor and Åse dived into one

of the lockers – she only just fitted. Lars opened the lid of one of the freezers, and the two of us grabbed Freddie and threw him in. We closed the lid so quickly he had to duck. That left Lars and me. I opened the other freezer lid – it was so cold that white smoke billowed out.

"Get in!" said Lars.

"And you?"

"There's space by the lockers," said Lars.

I got in and Lars dropped the lid.

I was plunged into a world of profound cold and blackness. It was far worse than falling in the lake – I was sealed in. I could barely move, there was so little room. And it was *so* cold. I tried to breathe in tiny sips, partly because the little blades of frozen air hurt my lungs and partly because I had to be careful: there wasn't much oxygen.

How long could I last? What were the guards doing?

I tried to listen, but I could only hear the hum of the freezer's motor.

A cold, lonely time passed – seconds felt like minutes, minutes felt like hours. Soon there was almost no air left.

I couldn't take it any more. I tried to push the lid open just a crack, but it wouldn't move. I tried again. It was too heavy.

I closed my eyes, thinking that if the others were going to find my corpse, at least I wouldn't be staring at them.

Finally – thank mercies! – the lid was raised and I opened my eyes to find Lars and Åse looking down at me.

They grabbed my arms and started to haul me out.

"What took you so long?" I asked, breathing in sobs. I was amazed that I could speak at all.

"Sorry," said Åse. "The guards went and talked to that chap for a bit. Then they wandered round the corridor for a minute or two before they went out again."

"Is Freddie OK?"

"He'll be fine. His freezer wasn't on," said Lars.

I felt as though I needed to rest for at least a week, but as soon as Lars had hauled Freddie out of his freezer, we had to get on with the job. We walked briskly down the corridor. Outside the door to the heavy water store we paused for a second.

The sign on the door said:

NO ADMITTANCE EXCEPT ON BUSINESS

"Well, that's all right," muttered Lars. "We're on business."

The door was unlocked. Freddie and I went in first, both pointing our Tommy guns at the old workman at the table.

"On your feet. Hands up," I said in English. Whatever happened, we had to pretend not to understand Norwegian.

The workman gave a start of surprise. He took off his glasses and stumbled to his feet, putting his hands in the air. He had a kindly, crumpled face. In fact he looked a bit like my uncle Mathias.

"Nothing will happen to you if you do as you're told. We're British army." I pointed to the embroidered insignia on the front of my camouflage suit.

But the workman's eyes were on Åse. How he was gawping at her! He was clearly wondering how old she was.

I had to get him out of our way.

"We're British army," I said again coldly. "Now, *move!*" I had both hands on the gun, so I gestured with a flick of my head that he was to go and stand by the wall.

I kept the gun trained on the old man as he moved, and Freddie took up position by the door.

Åse and Lars made for the table. Pushing the workman's papers aside, they laid out the eighteen plastic explosives. They were strange-looking things – grey, sausage-shaped lengths of putty-like stuff about a handspan in length. Each had what looked like a piece of candle wick attached to one end – the detonator fuse.

Lars and Åse put on rubber gloves and set to work on the heavy water cells at the far end of the room. They worked like a pair of old pros, quickly wrapping the explosives round each cell in turn. They always put the explosive in the same place – just below the water jacket, where the mechanism was most vulnerable. The explosives fitted snugly – they were exactly the right length. Even though I knew they were going as quickly as they could, the wait was agonizing.

The old workman watched Lars and Åse attentively, and when he saw exactly where they were placing the explosives, he nodded, as if to say "well done". When they were about halfway through he gave a polite cough.

"Excuse me," he said, "but I think you should know that there's a lye leakage. It's caustic, so be careful not to get any on your skin or clothing."

"Thank you," said Lars, who was crouched down low over a cell.

Åse shot him a smile. I did, too, relieved that he was speaking to us in English, not Norwegian.

Åse moved lickety-split down her row of cells. She finished first and started coupling the fuses in twos so that there'd be only nine fuses to ignite. Eight of these fuses she kept long – the fuse cord would burn at a rate of one centimetre per second. These fuses would take two minutes to go off, and were our back-up plan. The ninth fuse she cut much shorter – it was to detonate after only thirty seconds. She then linked the short fuse to the other detonators so as to set off all eighteen charges simultaneously.

Once the fuses were lit we would have thirty seconds to make our getaway. That wouldn't be long enough for us to leave the compound – we might not even get out of the building.

Åse quickly checked that the explosives were securely wrapped around the cells, then turned to me.

"Everything's set. OK to go?" she asked.

I thought for a moment. I was worried. What was I going to do with this nice old workman? We could hardly take him with us. I decided I'd let him run up the spiral staircase and get as far away from the explosion as possible. That was his best bet – as long as the building stood up to the blast.

Still pointing the Tommy gun, I walked the workman over to the door. Then I nodded to Lars, who lit a match and made for the fuses.

"Wait, please!" cried the workman. "My glasses! They're on the table. I need them for my job. They're impossible to replace these days."

"Get them," I said to Lars.

Lars blew out the match. The spectacle case was lying there with all the workman's crumpled-up papers on the edge of the table. Lars grabbed the case, dashed across the room and handed it to the man.

"Tusen takk," said the workman. I tried to read his expression. Why had he reverted to Norwegian? Was it just nerves?

Lars struck a second match. And he was just crouching down to light the first fuse when the workman cried out again.

"My glasses! They are not in the case!"

Again Lars blew out his match.

For a moment I shut my eyes. I couldn't believe what was happening. Nothing could be more important than what we were doing. Everything – the war, the future of the world, our own survival – hung in the balance. And we were worrying about an old man's glasses!

I was feeling really frantic.

"Where *are* your glasses?" I snapped.

The poor workman shrugged.

I held my breath while Lars and Åse rifled desperately through the papers on the table. If a guard came down the stairs and found us now…

Finally Lars opened a ledger and found a pair of delicate, metal-rimmed spectacles. He ran across the room and pressed the glasses into the workman's hand.

The old man looked at him intently and said, in Norwegian, "I've seen you before. You're one of the Petersens, aren't you?"

Lars looked at him, aghast.

This was disastrous!

"No!" I hissed at the workman. "We are British army agents. Remember that."

The old man nodded.

"Let's get a move on," I said.

Lars struck a third match and bent over to light the fuse.

That was when we heard footsteps coming down the stairs.

Everybody froze, even the workman, and Lars blew out the match.

We waited. I still had my gun on the workman, while Freddie and Åse were pointing theirs at the top rung of the spiral staircase.

The steps clanged noisily with every footfall. I took a deep breath in. Should we kill the guard to silence him? Would the noise raise the alarm?

Yet the footsteps were approaching at a most unhurried pace. It wasn't a good clipped soldier's march, but more of a slow shuffle.

"It'll be Gunnar," murmured the old workman.

"Who?" I asked.

"The nightwatchman," explained the workman. "He's a good Norwegian."

That was excellent news – a good Norwegian meant

someone who wasn't a Nazi sympathizer. So this man wouldn't shout out, or make things difficult.

But you could never be sure.

"Hands up! Stop where you are!" I cried as the man reached the bottom step.

The nightwatchman gave a start, put up his hands and blinked. One look at him in his old overalls and I knew he was no threat. He was just a gentle soul who mended dripping taps, and I felt sorry to be giving him such an unpleasant shock.

But there wasn't time to apologize, or to explain. I turned to the old workman and gestured to him to join Gunnar at the bottom stair.

"Right," I said. "When I shout 'go', run up the stairs as fast as you can. You should reach the second floor before the explosion. I'll follow once I've seen you up."

I could see Åse understood – I had to wait behind just in case one of the men put out the fuses. It was unlikely; they didn't look the sort. Instead I'd got a more serious worry: they were both old men and didn't look very fit. Would they be able to run up those stairs fast enough? I hoped they'd make it to safety. I hoped we all would.

I nodded to Lars and he lit the long fuses. I pressed the button on my stopwatch.

We waited.

We wouldn't leave the basement until the thirty-second fuse was lit. And that minute and a half seemed to last an eternity. The fuses hissed and sizzled and the stopwatch counted off the seconds at a slow plod.

Twenty-eight … twenty-nine…

Anything could happen now. What if someone had found the sabotaged gate?

Forty-three … forty-four…

Maybe an ambush was waiting for us outside that steel door?

Seventy … seventy-one…

At ninety seconds, Lars lit the short fuse, then dashed to the steel door with Freddie and Åse. I stayed behind. I counted aloud slowly – as if overseeing a race. The two men looked very anxious.

"Seven … eight … nine … ten … run!" and the old men clattered off up the stairs.

I sprinted down the hallway to the steel door. The others were already out in the yard running back the way we had come.

Only fifteen seconds remained. We had to get clear of the electrolysis building before the explosion.

I ran like I'd never run before, feet pounding against the ground. In the moonlight I could see Lars up ahead, crossing the open yard by the barracks.

I reached the yard, running blindly.

I wouldn't have time to make it to the gate. Not even Lars could have done that. The blast would come any moment now...

I leapt the last few paces and slid to a stop behind the storage tanks, where Freddie was already crouched down. I could see Lars and Åse behind some old drum casks.

I hunched my shoulders and waited for the big bang. But what came was more of a muffled thud, as if two steamrollers had collided. There was a flash of orange and then a splintering crash of breaking glass as the basement windows were blown out.

That was all. The sensible part of me was relieved. The electrolysis building hadn't collapsed. The workmen – and even that wretched pair of glasses – would be all right.

But I did feel a little *disappointed*.

The explosion hadn't been very dramatic. After all of the training in Scotland, and those endless, freezing weeks up on the plateau, and all the dangers and hardships that we'd faced...What had it all been for? It was silly, but I'd expected – at the very least – to be personally flattened by the blast.

For a moment it was as if nothing had happened. There were no sirens, no screams or shouts, no bursts of gunfire. All we could hear was the whistle of the wind and the hum of the machinery.

Then the door to the barracks opened and out stepped a German soldier, pulling on his greatcoat as he came. The man was bare-headed and unarmed – all he carried was a large torch. He glanced around the empty yard and then he shone his torch at the upper storeys of the electrolysis building. The torchlight moved slowly along the tiers of balconies on the top two floors of the building. If he lowered his torch just a fraction he'd see all those broken windows.

But it's extraordinary what someone can miss!

The guard didn't lower his torch. He just shook his head and made his way back to the barracks.

"You know why he was looking up at the balconies," whispered Freddie. "That's where they keep the gas burners that isolate the deuterium from the hydrogen. It's all highly combustible. Every time there's a glitch in the gas supply or—"

"Shhh!" I hissed.

The guard was back. He came out of the barracks again, and this time he had a gun. He clearly wasn't that worried, for he was holding his rifle loosely in his left hand, just like you might carry a garden spade.

The guard wandered across the yard towards the storage tanks, shining his torch from side to side.

I tensed my finger on the trigger. Once there was

gunfire the game would almost certainly be up. The soldiers would spill out of the barracks long before we could get near the gate.

I watched the guard as he shone his torch across the sky in a dreamy way. There was nothing I could do. In a desperate, last-ditch attempt, I screwed up my face and concentrated with all my might on wishing this blessed man back into his barracks.

But of course he didn't go away. The guard walked closer, until he was level with the flank of the storage tanks. Then he swung his torch in a wide arc round the yard and over the top of the tanks. If the beam of light moved the tiniest bit lower, he would see us.

Åse was nearest to him, her gun at the ready. *Shall I fire?* she mouthed.

I shook my head – *not yet.*

The guard hesitated. Then, quite unaware that his life was at stake, he trudged back into his barracks and closed the door.

I was so relieved that I wanted to pick Freddie up and hug him. Instead I waited thirty seconds and then gave a thumbs up. We ran out of the yard, through the gate (where Lars carefully draped the chain and padlock back into position), and down the railway track.

We didn't stop for breath until we got to the tree

by the cliff edge where we'd left the rope. Here I bent down and looked over the side into blackness. The wet rock face glistened faintly but I couldn't see the end of the rope. I knew it was only 50 metres long – it would only get us a fraction of the way down. I remembered the terrible climb up.

"Let's go on," I said, trying to sound confident. "There must be somewhere easier."

Freddie beamed with relief.

We untied the rope and set off running and stumbling through the snow.

A couple of hundred metres further down the track we came to a bare slope covered in slushy, melting snow. Here there were no trees or bushes to hold on to, so it would have been harder to climb than the cliff. However, the descent was more gradual with the mountain falling away in a series of steep slopes. Every so often there were little ledges which I hoped would break our descent.

We had to be quick; any moment now the sirens would go off, the spotlights would shine down and we'd be caught.

I went first. The fastest way was to slide down on our backsides – we'd get completely sodden, but at this point it didn't really matter. So I sat down on the edge of the mountain and pushed off. *Wheeeeeeeeeee…*

It was like vertical skiing. I just plummeted downwards. I tried using my hands to break my fall, but it was no use. Nothing could stop me.

I went faster and faster – a sort of human landslide – until I crashed to a halt at the first ledge, a hair's breadth from the edge of a ten-metre drop. I shuffled sideways several metres and set off again, angling myself diagonally across the slope. This time it was better. I stopped, changed direction, and took off again.

And so, sliding and slipping and stopping, I zigzagged my way down the mountainside, never quite sure in the darkness whether I was going to stumble over a cliff.

Soon my bottom half was completely soaked and the seat of my trousers was shredded by the rocks. But it was all over very quickly and I tumbled to a complete stop at the foot of the gorge.

While I waited for the others to come bumping down behind me, I inspected the river. We were in luck! Several huge blocks of ice had become stuck at a narrow point and, because they were all jammed up together, some had been pushed upwards to form a great white pile of ice in the middle of the river. The pile was unsteady, but it would make for a far easier crossing than last time.

Åse and Freddie went first, then Lars, then me.

I was half way across, balancing on the big ice pile, when a loud, blaring, deafening, horrendous screech nearly knocked me off my feet.

The siren.

The noise was nerve-jangling and loud. It throbbed on and on. Soon the spotlights would go on and they'd pick us off. Easy as shooting rats in a barrel.

When I got to the far bank of the river, Lars and Åse and Freddie were already starting up the cliff face. We had to get out of the gorge as fast as we could. Fear cleared our minds, and hand after hand, foot after foot we climbed and clambered in the darkness, pulling at the small trees and shrubs to lever ourselves up. The snow was very slushy – but we were so soaked that it didn't matter now. And, anyway, there was no time to rest and get cold.

We never stopped. My lungs were fighting for breath, but I just continued saying to myself, "Keep going, keep going. It's not far now, keep going."

And soon what I wished *did* come true. Up above me I saw the flicker of headlights weaving in and out of a dark line of trees. It couldn't be far to the road – ten or fifteen metres. One last ascent and we'd be out of the gorge.

When I reached the foot of the last climb the others were already a little way ahead. I paused for a second to adjust the straps on my rucksack. And at that moment there was a scraping sound and a shower of stones rained down all around me. A horrible, high-pitched scream filled the air. I covered my head with my hands and a body landed with a thud on the ledge beside me.

It was Freddie.

He lay there cold and limp as a fish. I crouched down at his side. At least he was breathing.

"Freddie?"

Nothing.

"FREDDIE!"

Still nothing.

"FREDDIE!"

I shouted in his ear, and gave him a sharp tap on the face.

Freddie let out a tiny grunt, but he didn't open his eyes.

I tried to remember my first aid. There was no blood, his airways seemed clear. Had he broken his back?

"Can you move your legs?"

Freddie let out another grunt, which seemed more of a "yes" grunt than a "no" grunt. But his body had gone all floppy and he seemed to be slipping away again…

I gave him a shake. The effect was instant. Freddie let out a moan of pain and opened his eyes. He looked up at me, his eyes unfocused and his breathing juddery.

"Just leave me," he said in a faint, faraway voice. "I'll be all right."

"We'll do nothing of the sort," I said briskly. "We can't leave you here for the Germans to find. And you know perfectly well you *won't* be all right with them!"

Lars and Åse were back on the ledge now. Lars quickly retrieved Freddie's glasses. Åse crouched over and unbuttoned Freddie's jacket. She checked him for injuries.

"Come on, Fred. You've bumped your head a bit, but it's not that bad. Sit up," she said.

I held one side of him and Åse the other and slowly we raised him up into a sitting position. He moaned as we moved him. His face was white and clammy.

"My arm," he murmured. "I can't move it."

At this point Åse tilted her head to one side and inspected Freddie's upper body. She was assessing him – it was the same shrewd look I once saw her give a climbing wall she was about to scale at Drumincraig.

"It's not your arm you've done in," she said. "It's your shoulder. You've dislocated it. Look." She pulled back the top of Freddie's coat. "His right shoulder – it's all out of shape and droopy. That arm'll be useless."

"How do you know this?" I asked.

She gave a shrug. "It happens all the time at the gym – people falling badly off the bar. He'll need to have it pulled back into place. Shall we do it now?"

"NO!" Freddie's voice was suddenly very loud and firm.

Lars looked over at me and I nodded. I held Freddie round the chest and Åse pressed her scarf into Freddie's mouth.

"Bite!" she hissed.

And as Freddie bit Lars took the bad arm and moved it firmly up and forward, swivelling the bone back into the socket. There was a muffled cry from Freddie and his eyes blazed. But the moment was quickly over and he slumped back in my arms.

"It'll come out again if he's not careful," warned Åse.

"We don't have time to rest now, Freddie,' I said. "We'll have to strap you up."

I took off my scarf and tied Åse's scarf to it, then I bound the material round poor Freddie, pinning his injured arm to his chest. He tried not to groan too much. But he did say, rather mournfully, "It's no good. How can I climb?"

"I'll carry you," said Lars. "Strap him to me, Jakob. Use the rope."

Åse and I lifted the groaning Freddie on to Lars's back and wound the rope round and round to fix him in place. Then Lars, laden down with Freddie, started to scale the rock face. I came up behind. I was amazed at Lars's strength – Freddie looked so heavy and awkward to carry, far worse than any of Colonel Armstrong's rucksacks full of stones.

Lars went slowly, stopping every minute or two before heaving himself and Freddie up a little further … and a little further … and a little further. I muttered encouragement from behind. Freddie kept his eyes squeezed shut the whole time.

At last we got to the road. Behind a cluster of trees, we untied the ropes around Lars and helped Freddie back onto his feet. Slowly and clumsily he staggered along beside us.

We crept up to the side of the road but, just as we were about to cross, a lorry came around the corner, splashing water everywhere. We ducked down and watched it pass. Sitting in the back was a platoon of German soldiers.

When the lorry disappeared we dashed over the road, Åse and I half lifting, half dragging Freddie along.

On the far side, we waded through a high bank of slushy snow and then, pushing briars and bushes aside, made our way up into the woods.

We came to a narrow trail leading through the trees and there the going got easier. But Freddie kept slowing down and stumbling, so I walked by his side, propping him up with one arm and trying to dream up nice things to whisper in his ear.

But he was a worry. I could see the pain was tiring him out. How on earth was he going to survive the journey into Sweden? Would he even make it as far as the hut?

After half an hour we reached the old power line road and came once again to the clearing where we had hidden our skis. We moved back the brushwood and hoisted our skis on to our shoulders. I took Freddie's skis as well as my own and he was in so much pain that I don't think he even noticed.

I cast a last glance back over the valley. Below us, I could see the headlights of more trucks, no doubt full of German soldiers, making their way along the road to Vemork. But on the far side of the gorge the power station was still in darkness. That was strange.

"The valley should be lit up. Why haven't they turned the floodlights on?" I asked the others.

"Look!" exclaimed Lars. He pointed to some tiny lights moving on the far side of the gorge, just to the west of the power station.

"That's a search party moving down the railway line," said Åse. "They're on our trail."

I turned to Freddie. The sight of his whey-coloured face and half-closed eyes filled me with dread. I gave him what I hoped was an encouraging smile.

"OK. The hunt is on."

Åse Jeffries

5TH JANUARY 1943

The Germans were really after us. So we moved fast – the kind of pace you go when there's somebody mad and angry lolloping up behind you with a meat cleaver.

It wasn't possible to go back to the hut the way we'd come – the snow was now too soft for us to climb straight up the mountainside. Instead we had to continue along the power line road and zigzag up the mountain, just under the cable car track, and come out on the plateau.

To make matters worse, the road wasn't really a road, but more like a shallow river. Everything was damp and squishy – not only the snow, but our gloves, our trousers, our spirits and – most of all – Fred's willpower.

The cruellest joke of all was the cable car just over our heads. It doesn't work in the winter, but it would have taken nothing to get it going. Just a touch of lubricating oil, a spot of diesel, press one little red button and we'd have been at the top in a flash.

There was also the other small matter of imminent death. Apart from a few trees along the edge, the cable car road was completely exposed. If the Germans sent a few trucks into the mountains they'd pick us up sure as fudge cupcakes are fudge cupcakes. And why didn't they? Were we just *too* obvious? I couldn't understand why the troops were running around Vemork like blind white mice, pawing their way foot by foot along the railway track. Why didn't they look on the other side of the gorge? And why didn't some noodle brain think to turn on the cable car lights?

Well, thank God they didn't, because it saved our skins!

We struggled up that steep uphill slope like a line of pilgrims, hauling our skis on our backs and never stopping, except to help Fred on. He kept flagging and Jakob ended up walking by his side, clucking like a mother hen, telling him always that there were just one or two more corners and then we'd be there.

Long after we thought it would never happen, we turned one more corner and we *were* at the top. We stood on that ridge, looking out at the snow and the rock and the sky of the plateau. Even though the search parties were probably gathering down in the valley, we had to stop for a moment. It's kind of strange, but I felt I was back in our land. It might have been grim and dangerous and cold, cold, *cold*, but the Hardanger belonged to us.

And then, of course, the two things that had been about to go horribly wrong *did* go horribly wrong.

The first thing was Fred, but we didn't notice him wander off because we were too busy looking up at the other thing which was going wrong, and that was the sky.

It was building up for a storm and the air was becoming strangely dense and solid – as if the atmosphere was a huge upended bowl hanging over us. As we watched, the sky started to change – subtly yellowing the way milk does as you churn it into butter.

Then Jakob said, "Where's Freddie?"

We looked all round. He'd *vanished*!

We set out in three different directions – it made me recall that time after the landing when we were trying to find those coffin-shaped boxes in the snow.

As Fred was in his camouflage suit, he too was white all over.

I found him only twenty metres away, curled up in the snow, snug as an Arctic fox.

"Fred! Get up!"

He made a snuffling sound.

"Fred!" I gave him a prod.

"Just go on," he said in a slurry voice, not even bothering to open his eyes.

"Fred, you can't stay here!"

"Just go on. You don't need me."

"Yes we do! You're our brains! We wouldn't have found that tunnel into the basement without you. Get up! You can't just lie there! You've got to keep moving!"

He gave a faint smile. "I am moving," he replied. "I may seem still. But I'm orbiting the sun at 104,000 kilometres an hour. And so are you."

I grabbed Mr Infuriating-Know-It-All by his good arm and tried to shake him to his senses. But then I realized that his eyes were swimming and his breath smelt sweet and chemical. A piece of gauze fell out of his hand.

The chloroform.

"Just thought I'd help you out," he said. And with that his head sank back into the snow.

"You idiot!" I blurted.

Jakob and Lars had just reached me and I showed them the piece of gauze.

"Chloroform," I said. "That stuff can kill. It can stop your heart just like *that*!" I meant to click my fingers together, but my gloves were too soggy.

Jakob's face was creased with worry. "I'm sure that was his intention," he said quietly.

That made me feel terrible. Jakob was right – Fred must have felt he was holding us back. I should have been more sympathetic.

There was no time for regrets. We already had a weird streaky-bacon sky, with great bands of red and yellow cloud. As the air darkened around us, we followed Jakob's instructions and built a stretcher using ski poles and clothing and rope. Then we bundled Fred up in every bit of clothing we could find. Lars took one end and Jakob the other and we set off across the plateau.

Then the weather closed in. *Bam!* The temperature dropped and a stinging cold wind of snow and flying ice hit us hard. But at least it was blowing from behind us – pushing us forward. We took turns with the stretcher. After carrying the skis and the explosives, Fred didn't seem so very heavy, but we had to ski carefully to synchronize our movements.

We had ages until we reached our old hut. We couldn't stop at yesterday's hut – that was too close to Vemork. Instead we were heading through this white wind to our old, rickety hut – the one with the holes in the planking and only two chairs and the reindeer skins on the floor.

We just went on and on, groping our way along, pushed by the wind, thinking: *hut, fire, food, sleep. Hut, fire, food, sleep. Hut, fire, food, sleep.*

It took us three hours to cross the plateau, but they weren't like normal clock hours. The wind and our tiredness and our fear distorted everything and made the time warp and curl up at the edges like an old railway station sandwich.

In the end we *did* reach the hut. When we got in,

Lars laid a fire in the stove, using some of those awful angling magazines as kindling.

We've put Fred nearest the stove and now we're all in our sleeping bags. Nobody can face cooking, so we've got out a little pemmican and are chewing it raw – something I could never have done a few weeks ago. I've just whispered "food" in Fred's ear, but he hasn't woken up. I never thought I'd see the day that he passed up an opportunity to eat.

I'm going to settle down now for a few hours' sleep. We can't do anything until the storm dies down. Nor, I'm glad to say, can the Germans. So, for once, it's quite comforting to hear that caterwauling outside. I know that even if the hut shakes like a handkerchief in a gale, the walls will hold. And, as nobody in their right minds will set out in this weather, the storm is protecting us and giving us time to rest. Maybe the elements really *are* on our side.

Åse Jeffries

6TH JANUARY 1943

I woke very early this morning. The little window was iced over and Lars and Fred (very pale but – thank God! – still alive) were still asleep. The storm was snoozing too – the hut wasn't shaking any longer and all that was left was a high-pitched whistle of wind.

Jakob had clearly been up for ages. He was itching to be away.

He also had his In-Charge voice on.

"Åse, you and Lars will have to make that journey into Sweden on your own. I'll stay and get help for Freddie. He can't make that journey in the state he's in now."

Well, I wasn't having any of that!

"Don't be ridiculous," I said. "I'll stay with Fred."

"It's my duty. I'm meant to be responsible for everybody," intoned Jakob.

"Stuff your duty," I replied. "You and Lars are far stronger than me. *You* go to Sweden. I probably couldn't keep up anyway. I never thought we'd get through yesterday. But now that we have, I rather fancy the idea of staying alive."

Jakob gave a mirthless laugh, but I wasn't being ironic.

"Think about it, Jakob." (He's not the only one who can be bossy...) "I'm much better suited to this than you. The Germans are going to be on the lookout. And consider what an improbable combination Fred and I make: knobbly-kneed Fred and a *girl*. The Germans may think it possible that the Brits sent in underage troops to crawl up cliffs, but a *girl*? And a midget of a girl like me?"

Lars was sitting up now. And, just for once, he spoke up. "She's right, Jakob," he said.

There was a tense pause while Jakob thought things through. Then he sighed.

"OK," he said. "Åse goes with Freddie. And we'll meet up again in Stockholm."

"There're some excellent cafés in Stockholm," said a bleary voice from down by the fire.

Fred was awake!

"There's one in Skaningen with a little red sign of a cat outside. They do truffled chicken soup and calf's tongue with sweetbreads, and hot chocolate with warm raisin bread and solvag slice, fruit tarts…"

When Fred had rattled off the menu, we agreed that when, or if (and it's a big "if"!), we get to Stockholm, we'll meet up in his little red cat café. We'll go there every afternoon at three o'clock and if the café is closed we'll meet at the pancake house on the other side of the square.

As for the journey, Jakob thinks it'll take him and Lars about ten days to get across the border. They've checked their addresses in Stockholm against Fred's super-accurate database brain, but I have no idea how or when or even if Fred and I will get out. We certainly won't be as quick as them. And Fred's shoulder is going to take weeks to heal properly.

According to Lars, there's an inn in Rjukan, though he doesn't know if the owner is an informer. Its about a day's travel from here and Fred and I think we should go straight there, check into a room, and – once we're cleaned up – go and have a nice hot meal in the dining room.

I know this all sounds like madness, because the whole place will be crawling with edgy, angry Germans on the look out for saboteurs. But sometimes the best place to hide from the enemy is directly under his nose. It's about keeping our nerve and remembering our manners. We'll have to eat nicely and use our napkins. That'll be hard – it's weeks since either of us ate at a table with a proper plate and knife and fork.

Fred and I are going to go back the way we came, skiing across the plateau south-south-east and then taking the cable car road down to the village. Fred thinks he'll be up to the trip. He still looks pale, but far better than yesterday. I've frisked him for chloroform pads, though. Just in case.

Jakob P. Stromsheim

This is my last entry before we set out on the overland journey for Sweden. I have no idea if I'm going to be able to keep going. We really haven't got enough food and there's so much that could go wrong. And so much too that I need to know. I still can't get Lars to tell me how he ended up with that button compass of Father's. I've tried and I've tried, but each time he clams up even more.

This morning, as we were getting ready to go, I sent one last message to London. The radio was a real fiddle to set up and I was nowhere near as quick as Freddie at tapping out Morse. So I kept my message short:

HIGH-CONCENTRATION INSTALLATION AT
VEMORK COMPLETELY DESTROYED STOP
ON THE WAY TO SWEDEN STOP

That sounded so simple – *on the way to Sweden*. But there's no "way", no straight road or route to Sweden. We had a map, but it only gave a vague outline of the land. We would have to rely on the compass and simply head out over the mountains and follow the rivers, until we came to the border.

Åse and Freddie were the first to leave the hut. It seemed so quiet without them, but I got on with hiding the transmitter under the floorboards and then Lars and I divided up the rest of the jobs.

Lars waxed the skis while I emptied the remains of the food shelf into the rucksacks. At the back of the shelf there was a horrible tin of golden syrup. It was stuck to the shelf and looked centuries old. All round the rim there was a foul black crust of dead ants.

I don't know how Lars knew about the tin – I suppose we've all been keeping a very close eye on the stores – but without even looking up from what he was doing he just said, "Take it. Take the syrup."

"It's heavy and it's full of ants! Even Freddie hasn't touched it."

"Pack it all the same. You never know."

I paused. We were 400 kilometres from the border. If I'd come round to eating semi-digested moss and reindeers' eyeballs, I could surely crunch my way through a few caramelized ants.

I packed the jar.

Now we had to get on our way.

Jakob P. Stromsheim

7TH JANUARY 1943

I'm in a small, windy cave somewhere on the Hardanger Plateau. This is written after two nights with no sleep.

I'm scribbling this with the log on my knees – there's no flat surface. These are what the Colonel might call "suboptimal conditions". Could I be missing his sour old sense of humour?

Two days ago we set off north-east from the hut. The snow was crisp and there was only an occasional flurry of wind to slow our progress. We crossed over a series of wide valleys and we could hear aircraft – the Germans were clearly sending in search parties. Sometimes we saw the planes circling far off like noisy birds. When they came near we took cover behind a rock or an overhang – we assumed that if we could see someone, they could see us too.

These stops didn't hold us back much. Lars knew this part of the plateau from two years ago when – so he told me – he'd helped hide some small arms caches in a hut about sixty kilometres east of Vemork.

By early afternoon we reached a hut at Lake Skryken and I was feeling quite happy as I shook off my skis and made for the door.

But the latch was open.

I took off my goggles, and stepped inside. Immediately, all the blood in my body plummeted to my boots. Someone had been here before us … someone that was *not* a friend.

The mattresses had been pulled from the bunks and slashed open. The table and chairs were upturned, and someone had broken into the cupboard, pulled the drawers out and ripped open the bags of tea and sugar. There were books and charts strewn everywhere across the floor.

For a second we gawped at it all uselessly, but then I saw something *very* scary. By the stove there were lumps of snow that must have come off the tracks of someone's boots. The lumps were still unmelted. The visitors had *only just left*!

We ran outside and scanned the landscape. We didn't need binoculars. To the east, less than a kilometre away, five German soldiers were skiing towards the hut at top speed. They seemed to be spanning out to encircle us.

We put on our skis. I never knew I could get them on so fast.

"Into the sun!" cried Lars. And he pushed off so hard on his ski poles that they made a twanging sound.

The soldiers hadn't closed in completely – there were still gaps between them. And Lars dived into one of these gaps. I followed, skiing faster and harder than I ever thought I could. And at the same time I was groping for that little capsule in my trouser pocket. Lars might make it – he's a far faster skier – but *me* against *five grown men*?

I charged forward into the low afternoon sun. The light was dazzling, so I kept my head down and pushed, following Lars's track. For all I knew we could be heading straight for a cliff, but what did it matter? At least a couple of Germans would die with us.

Out of the corner of my eye, I saw the two soldiers nearest to us stop. They were going to fire. I skied on – better to be a moving target.

I heard the gunshots – two loud cracks, a third crack, and then, very quickly, a fourth. With four shots, I couldn't believe they hadn't hit me, but I seemed to be OK.

I screwed up my eyes to see Lars pounding ahead just as fast as before. He hadn't been hit either. Lars was right to ski into the sun: no one could aim accurately with the light in their eyes.

But the Germans were not giving up. I reached the brow of a hill and looked back. The five men were climbing up the slope. And they were moving fast!

Down, down I went into a shallow, rocky valley and then up over a small ridge and out onto a lakeside plateau. I glanced back and saw that one of the soldiers had fallen behind and was doubled over his ski poles.

One down, four to go.

The next time I looked back there were only three Germans. A few minutes later we were down to two, but what a pair! They were very, very determined. And they were good skiers, faster on the uphill than us, though Lars and I seemed to gain a bit on the descents. Perhaps that was because we took more risks – we had nothing to lose.

Gradually, though, they were closing in on us. Soon they were right behind me. And everything was drawing to a close. I was coming to the end of my strength.

Even if we were scared out of our wits, we couldn't ski on for ever. Something had to give.

We came to the head of the next pass and then Lars suddenly put on a new spurt of speed. I followed, cutting out every twist and turn that I could. If we raced down this mountainside fast enough, the momentum should take us a good way up the other side of the valley.

So I roared down the hill and, thirty metres up the far slope of the valley, I came to a stop. I swivelled round quickly and started sidestepping fast up the mountainside, trying to stop the poles from sinking too deeply into the snow. As I went, I grappled my Colt .32 pistol out of the waistband of my trousers and put it in my pocket.

Lars was a good way ahead. Then a minute later he was out of sight over the brow of the mountain. I glanced across the valley. We were down to one German now. The other had taken a fall and was lying very still in the snow on the far slope. But the remaining soldier was just forty metres away.

"Hände hoch!" he shouted.

I stopped, grabbed my pistol and turned.

The German suddenly stood up very straight – he'd seen that I was armed. Even if my Colt .32 wasn't much of a match for his Luger.

I held my arm out very straight. It was too far to shoot at all accurately, but I pointed the gun at his chest and shot.

I missed.

The German fired back twice, but too quickly. Both shots were wide.

I was just about to shoot again, when I realized something important. This was a battle of nerves – for we were pretty well out of range of each other. In a duel like this, it would be the man with no bullets left who lost.

The German would have – at most – six bullets in his Luger. So only four shots to go. He fired again. I flinched. This was a waiting game. If I was wounded, I knew exactly where the capsule was and what I had to do.

I heard the Luger crack again. Two shots to go. I tried to think reassuring thoughts. Maybe the German would have sweat in his eyes... Maybe his arm muscles would be too tense.

A bullet whirred past my elbow.

He wasn't too tense.

One shot left. The German was honing his range and each successive shot had come a little nearer. With this final bullet he'd be able to strike home.

I didn't know why I was standing still and making

it easy for him. I should have been moving. I was a sitting duck!

Then I realized I wasn't quite as still as I thought – I was shaking. And just while I was wondering whether to duck, the German shot for the final time. The bullet passed so close I felt the air graze my cheek. It made a pinging noise as it ricocheted off a rock right behind me.

His last bullet. Now he was mine! The German looked down at his gun barrel, turned and started skiing frantically back down the mountainside.

I set off after him, getting closer and closer. The shoot-out had been like standing before a firing squad and now I didn't know if I had the concentration to aim properly. But that was no excuse – he was easily within range now.

I stopped, aimed my Colt and fired two shots.

Nothing happened.

Then, from somewhere, a third shot rang out and the man gave a scream and crumpled to the ground.

I looked at my gun, confused. I'd only pulled the trigger twice.

Then I heard the swish of skis behind me. A moment later, Lars came to a halt by my side.

"Got him in the leg," he said numbly. And he stared at the soldier lying there in the snow clutching his thigh, and whimpering.

"It was just one little flick of my finger," said Lars, his eyes glazed.

I was surprised – I thought Lars was made of sterner stuff. I did feel sorry for the German, but I didn't feel guilty. He would have killed us if he could have.

Anyway, there was no time for pity. We were still in danger. I tugged at Lars's jacket.

"Come on," I said. "We've got to get moving, or his friends will catch up with us."

As we were leaving, I looked back one last time – the man was still lying there, his body swaying back and forth with pain. There was no sign of the others.

By the time we reached the next valley the sun was a low yellow rim on the skyline. We stopped long enough to cut off some pemmican and then we set off again, chewing as we pushed on through the dusk. We had to hurry – soon the Germans would regroup and take up the chase again. Even in the dark they'd be able to follow our tracks.

When we reached Lake Vråjoen we didn't stop at the hut on the shore side – and we didn't look in for spare food. Instead we set off across the bare ice of the lake, towards a ridge of mountains on the far side. I knew that this ice wasn't quite as thick as Lars would've liked and that if it broke we'd both go under.

GUNS

Colt Model 1903 Pocket Hammerless
Colt Single Action Army
Luger PO8 Pistol
Thompson Submachine Gun
(Tommy Gun)

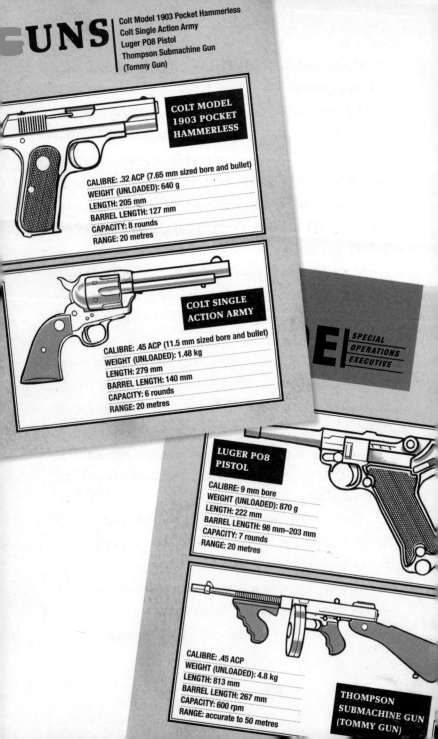

COLT MODEL 1903 POCKET HAMMERLESS

CALIBRE: .32 ACP (7.65 mm sized bore and bullet)
WEIGHT (UNLOADED): 640 g
LENGTH: 205 mm
BARREL LENGTH: 127 mm
CAPACITY: 8 rounds
RANGE: 20 metres

COLT SINGLE ACTION ARMY

CALIBRE: .45 ACP (11.5 mm sized bore and bullet)
WEIGHT (UNLOADED): 1.48 kg
LENGTH: 279 mm
BARREL LENGTH: 140 mm
CAPACITY: 6 rounds
RANGE: 20 metres

SPECIAL OPERATIONS EXECUTIVE

LUGER PO8 PISTOL

CALIBRE: 9 mm bore
WEIGHT (UNLOADED): 870 g
LENGTH: 222 mm
BARREL LENGTH: 98 mm–203 mm
CAPACITY: 7 rounds
RANGE: 20 metres

CALIBRE: .45 ACP
WEIGHT (UNLOADED): 4.8 kg
LENGTH: 813 mm
BARREL LENGTH: 267 mm
CAPACITY: 600 rpm
RANGE: accurate to 50 metres

THOMPSON SUBMACHINE GUN (TOMMY GUN)

But I'd run out of fear and it was a relief to be travelling over a surface that would hide our trail.

We travelled on over the lake and up the mountainside. It was dark now, so we had to go more slowly. And as we travelled I went over and over that gun battle with the German. I was so tired I don't really know how my legs kept going. We were half starved, for we hadn't eaten properly in days. And this was our second night with no sleep.

At dawn we reached the pass over one of the higher mountain ridges and we stopped to rest. It was *such* a relief.

We sat side by side on a great slab of granite looking back across the plateau. The hills and valleys beneath us were like a series of white waves. I took out our binoculars. There were no dark spots moving about. At *last*! No Germans.

But there was still one nasty doubt that had been nagging away at me all night. I had a question I had to ask Lars.

"Lars," I said. "Why did it take you so long to come back? Did you think you might just go on alone?"

"What?" He looked genuinely puzzled.

"When that German shot at me. It took ages for you to come back."

"I was just over the brow. I came back the second

I heard the gunfire. It was all over so fast."

"Fast?" It was my turn to look bewildered.

"Yes," said Lars. "He shot at you as if he was firing a submachine gun. All I heard was bang-bang-bang-bang-bang-bang."

"But ages passed between each of those shots. I stood there for ever!"

"That's just your mind playing tricks on you," replied Lars with a grim little smile. "Remember – everything changes up here on the plateau; not just light and weather, but time too."

"You mean it's not like the real world?" I couldn't quite understand what he was saying.

"No," he replied. "It's *more* real!"

Then he must have heard something, for he picked up the binoculars and started to scan the skyline.

Lars didn't have time to speak – he pulled me back with him behind the rock just in time. The next second, a small German army aircraft tore through the air. It swept down through the valley in a series of loops.

I poked my head round the side of the rock and looked down. It was strange – I'd never seen an aeroplane flying below me before.

"They're still after us," I said.

Lars nodded grimly.

The aircraft trailed off to the west. When the sound of the engine had died away, we put on our backpacks and set off.

Åse Jeffries

6TH JANUARY 1943

I'm writing this in a hotel room which smells of furniture polish and wet dog. Sadly I no longer have the sturdy, official-looking log to write in. I'm making do with a few scraps of paper that Jakob tore out for me before we parted. I hope that one day we'll get the chance to stitch the whole thing back together again.

In the hours that Fred and I spent making our way across the plateau, I prepared our cover story. By the time we got to Rjukan our account was long and elaborate and pretty well word-perfect. Oh boy! Were we going to need it.

Fred's shoulder was hurting the whole time we were skiing. I felt sorry for him, but we just had to keep going.

At the foot of the plateau, we abandoned our skis in the woods, and got to Rjukan just after six o'clock. It was dark and full of little narrow streets, all cobbles and puddles. There wasn't a soul in sight – not even one of those muffled-up old ladies in galoshes that you always see in Norwegian villages. I thought that there might be a curfew. Or was this what wartime Norway was always like?

We wandered down the main road until we found the inn Lars had told us about. There was a board by the front door displaying the menu and room prices. Inside we could hear noise – loud German voices and laughter.

Shucks! I'd said a lot of brave things to the others about the need to outface the enemy and stride into the lion's den. And Fred and I had agreed that we would go straight to the inn. But now I didn't feel quite so sure.

"I don't like this," I said. "Why don't we go on to the address in Miland?"

But Fred was reading the menu.

"They've got trout and potato croquettes," he announced, as if that decided everything.

"Trout or no trout, I still don't like it," I said. "It's full of Germans!"

"Well, so what if it is? We'll get a good supper," said Fred, sniffing the air like a bloodhound.

"But this could be the end of us!" I wailed.

"I don't care," said Fred. "My shoulder is killing me. Anyway, gluttony is my favourite deadly sin. If I don't die happy, at least I'll die full."

There was no stopping him. He pushed the door and went in. I followed. I really shouldn't have given in, but I did. There's something particularly humiliating about being defeated by a potato croquette.

Inside I knew immediately that it wasn't our sort of place. A nice big pair of swastika banners were hanging in the foyer. And by the little bell at the reception desk was a pile of *Fritt Folk* – that's the quisling newspaper – for sale.

We handed over our exquisitely forged passports (I'm Anne Fetja and Fred is Knut Halveson), paid a rather severe-looking lady for our night's lodgings and carried our rucksacks upstairs. We'd already made our first mistake – as good little collaborators we should have bought a *Fritt Folk*.

Our room was on the first floor with a bathroom to the side and a little balcony window over the front. We ran a bath – our first in months. BLISS! (Water afterwards *very* grimy.) But being a good citizen, I reused the soapy water to wash the clothes and underwear we'd worn every day for the last hundred years. (Bath water now indescribable…) I used the rope from our rucksack to make a washing line and I hung our wet clothes on pretty well every surface of the bedroom. We were really lowering the tone.

We changed into the civilian clothes which had been buried at the bottom of our rucksacks for weeks. I helped Fred into a checked shirt, traditional Norwegian jumper and trousers. He winced a lot when I moved his arm. All the same, when he was properly scrubbed-up, he looked OK-ish. But I had – wait for it – a *tweed skirt*. I hadn't worn a skirt for ages and I'd forgotten how draughty they are – particularly when you have little chicken legs like mine. The future for me is definitely going to be trousers.

Anyway, Mr Norwegian Sweater and Miss Chicken Legs then went downstairs to supper. We had trout and croquettes and winter greens and a sauce made from wild mushrooms. Pudding was also picked from the mountains: whortleberries in syrup on a sponge base. It was really nice – food on white china plates! Vegetables that weren't reindeer moss! Real coffee! (Also a sure sign that the hotel is collaborating with the Germans.)

Afterwards Fred complained that he still wasn't full and wanted to have the whole meal again, but I said no. We'd already drawn attention to ourselves by turning up without any adults. And besides (maybe Fred had never noticed this), normal people only eat *one* supper.

We went back upstairs. The bedroom had seemed so luxurious and comfortable when we first arrived but somehow we'd managed to mess everything up. Our hanging garden of dripping long johns and not-so-clean socks was giving off a decidedly biological smell, so I opened the windows. Fred said the food had made

265

him feel so much better he now had the strength to give his Colt .32 a long overdue clean.

I was just getting ready for bed and I'd already taken my shirt off when there was a sharp rap on the door.

"Wait a minute!" I called.

We were completely unprepared, but at least I had locked the door. I picked up my gun, stuck it in my waistband and then wrapped one of the big bath towels round me. Fred grabbed the bits of his gun off the bed and jammed them behind the wet washing.

I opened the door.

There were two men and an enormous pair of teeth standing there. The teeth belonged to the older man – I think he was the town sheriff. Behind him stood a German soldier in a long trench coat.

"Good evening!" said the sheriff. His smile was rather amazing – it managed to reach almost as far as his ears without going anywhere near his eyes.

"ID?" he asked.

Fred handed him his passport.

The sheriff quickly glanced at it and passed it back to the soldier.

"And your little girlfriend?" Those teeth again.

I handed him my passport. It was time to go on the offensive.

"I'm *not* his girlfriend. I'm his step-second-cousin once removed," I said indignantly.

"Sorry?" he said.

I spoke fast. "Knut is my aunt's older sister's step-grandson. My uncle Klaus's wife, Phoebe's sister Signy, married a widower with grown-up children, and Birgar, that's Knuttie's father, was one of them. So we aren't technically blood relatives – just members of the same extended family."

"I see," replied the sheriff. He didn't, but at least the smile was waning. "And what are you doing out here?"

"We're on a walking holiday," said Fred. "We've been

following the road from Skinnarbu, through Krokan."

That wasn't enough. The sheriff was still smiling, but his eyes were now flitting round the room. If he was any good he'd notice that our rucksacks were clearly foreign make. Worse still, Fred had left the cleaning rod and an oily rag on the bed.

We *had* to distract him. "Sir," I said heading towards the French windows, "on this holiday we've been learning about the stars. There are such wonderful skies up here in the mountains," I enthused. "And Knut's just a genius at them."

I gave Fred a prod-in–the-ass look. He got the message and led the two men out on to the balcony, pointing out the Pole Star, and Cassiopeia. By the time he reached Ursa Major he'd really got into his stride.

"Now if you follow the Belt of Orion – see that bright star. That's Aldebaran, a very interesting K5III star. It's a bit long in the tooth – it's used up most of its hydrogen and has mainly moved on to fusing helium. It's about 65 million light years away. So, in fact, even though it looks small, it's got a diameter 38 times greater than the sun – and shines 150 times more powerfully. It has a long-period radial velocity oscillation of about—"

"Fine, fine," said the sheriff, backing into the room again. "Glad you're enjoying yourselves."

But now he was looking at the laundry. Had he seen the gun parts?

He moved towards the wet long johns. I groped for my pistol. I'd have to shoot him if he went any closer.

"Do you mind!" I said, in a shocked voice. "That's my underwear over there!"

He blushed and looked flustered.

"I'm sorry, Miss Fetja." He paused.

It was a nasty little moment.

"What are you looking for anyway?" I asked bossily.

"Saboteurs," he said. "They've attacked the hydro plant."

"Oh!" I said, trying to sound shocked.

"Anyway," said the sheriff with a sigh. "Enjoy the rest of your holiday." He handed back the passports.

"Happy hunting," said Fred.

"Oh, I don't want to meet them," said the sheriff with a nervous laugh. "I hear they're armed."

You bet we are! I thought, as I closed the door.

Åse Jeffries

7TH JANUARY 1943

Sleeping in a real bed was wonderful, even with Fred tossing and turning and moaning away next to me.

But I was worried about the sheriff – might he have second thoughts? Might he get suspicious? I woke at six o'clock – three hours before dawn – and we quickly dressed in our civilian clothes.

Fred was feeling so poorly that he didn't mind skipping breakfast. He looked terrible. I asked him how his shoulder felt and he replied that at this point he wouldn't really care if his arm was chopped off.

We were just about to go when I heard the stutter of a car engine. I crept out to the balcony. Outside the inn, two men in boots and greatcoats were getting out of a large Chrysler. One of them was the sheriff!

Very quietly I closed the balcony door.

"Fred! The sheriff's here!"

We raced down the stairs, rucksacks on our backs, and dived through the green baize door into a long galley kitchen where a woman was crouched down by the oven. She looked up in surprise. I put my fingers to my lips and she smiled.

"Back door?" I whispered.

She gestured to a door at the side of the kitchen. It led to a crowded scullery with sheets hanging on a pulley. The doorbell rang. We clambered round some bales of dirty washing, crawled across the floor on our hands and knees and slid the bolt back on the door.

We came out into a paved courtyard and, with a little light from the kitchen window, we groped our way along a damp passageway from the back of the house and out on to the street. There was the sheriff's car, so he was still inside searching for us or questioning the innkeeper.

We scuttled up the dark street, Fred stumbling along behind me (I don't know how he did it), until we reached the bus stop. We were heading for the village of Miland where a family called the Froylands would help us. I knew there wouldn't be a bus until seven o'clock, but thankfully there were some big bins nearby and we huddled behind them and prayed that the sheriff would give us up for lost.

We spent a long cold half hour crouched up behind those bins. Fred was shivering and miserable and could only speak in little gasps and winces. Thank goodness we didn't try to ski to Sweden – he'd never have made it.

At about five to the hour, a couple of people arrived to wait at the bus stop and we sauntered out from behind the bins trying to look casual and relaxed (even though Fred could barely walk).

Once we were on the bus, things began to look up. The bus was warm and didn't jiggle Fred's shoulder too much. We got off at Miland and Fred had remembered the Colonel's notes and knew the directions to the Froylands' farmhouse, which was some way out of the town.

But he found the walking really hard. By the time we came off the road onto a dirt track, Fred was staggering. Then, just as I thought we were on the last lap – I could even see a farmhouse up ahead – he stumbled on something and crumpled to the ground. As he did so, he let out a terrible groan and I knew immediately that he'd put his shoulder out again.

I couldn't get him to move at all. I didn't know what to do. There was no one in sight, just Fred and me and the open fields with the mountains beyond. I crouched down and took hold of him round the ribs. He felt heavier than a piano, but I managed to haul him to his feet. Then I put his good arm round my shoulder and slowly – so very, very slowly – we hobbled down the track.

The farmhouse was trim and had a brass dolphin knocker on the front door. I knocked and a woman with one of those kind, snub-nosed currant-bun kind of faces opened the door.

"Mrs Froyland," I said. "We need help."

But she didn't look at me. She was staring at Fred. Just in time, she reached out her arms and caught him as he fainted.

Her eyes flicked over the fields behind us. "Quick," she said. "Inside."

She carried Fred into the kitchen and set him down on a rocking chair by the stove. The room was homely and neat with a scrubbed wooden table and crocheted cushions on the chairs. It made me long for home.

Mrs Froyland filled the kettle and sat down. The Colonel had said we were never to tell people what we'd been doing. It would only compromise them and make it harder if they were taken in for questioning. But I did feel I owed Mrs Froyland some sort of explanation.

"We've been living out in a hut on the Hardanger for a month," I said.

"Yes, I can see that," she replied calmly.

How on earth could she know that?

She must have seen the surprise on my face, because she smiled at me. "Your nails," she said. I looked down. Despite the bath last night my hands were still black with engrained dirt. So were Fred's.

Mrs Froyland continued, "And you're both bone thin. Normal children, even in wartime, aren't this skinny."

Fred lay half asleep on a rocking chair by the stove. Mrs Froyland gave him an appraising look.

"How long has his shoulder been out?"

"About twenty minutes," I said.

She raised her eyebrows in surprise.

"It isn't the first time," I explained. "He had a fall three days ago."

"That fits with the power station," she said.

I gave her a little half nod.

"But you're just kids!" she said, astonished.

I nodded again. And she smiled.

While we drank some tea, Mrs Froyland looked at Fred's shoulder. She said that maybe we hadn't got the joint properly back in the socket the first time. Then she went out and came back a few minutes later accompanied by a large man with a very similar, round, snub-nosed face.

"This is my brother, Haakon," she said.

Haakon grinned and rubbed his hands together. They were the size of paddles.

Mrs Froyland poured a glass of akvavit (it's a spirit a little like vodka) which she told Fred to drink, then she moved a pile of papers and all the crockery off the kitchen table. In Norway, it seems, the kitchen doubles as an operating theatre.

Mrs Froyland beckoned to Fred.

"Up on the table, lad. Haakon is going to see what he can do. Don't worry – you're in safe hands. He saves more lambs every year than any other farmer round here."

As Haakon took off his boots, Freddie very slowly climbed onto the kitchen table and lay down. He was so resigned to the pain that I don't think he was bothered about what lay ahead. But he closed his eyes. I don't think he wanted to see what was going to happen.

I wish I'd closed my eyes too.

Haakon looked carefully at the shoulder for a minute. He put his stockinged foot in Fred's armpit for leverage and picked up the bad arm. Then, with a powerful movement that would either rip the arm off entirely or slot it back into place, he jerked the limb backwards.

Fred gave a loud squeak, like a hundred guinea pigs meeting a fox on a dark night. Then he passed out.

"It's in," said Haakon.

When Fred had regained consciousness, Mrs Froyland brought out some bandages and bound his arm to his chest. She said he needed to remain like this for two or three days and afterwards he would have to wear a sling for a couple of weeks. She told us we couldn't sleep in the house. The Germans were doing regular house-to-house searches and it was too risky.

Haakon took us to a huge barn round the back of the house. There were bales of hay piled up in one corner and they looked rather comfortable. But Haakon smiled, shook his head and pointed upwards.

Far, far above us were the huge beams that supported the roof and, to judge by the droppings on the ground, acted as sleeping perches for hordes of bats. Resting on these beams were some narrow wooden planks – our sleeping perches. If we were to fall off it would be onto the cement floor.

Haakon rested one of his huge hands on my shoulder.

"Don't worry," he said gallantly. "If you do roll off, I've set plenty of bones before."

Then he brought out a rickety old ladder and we

climbed up – not at all easy for Fred, with his arm bound up. Nor is getting down very straightforward for him either.

The drill is that we climb up the ladder and then cast it to the far side of the barn – otherwise it would give away our hiding place. When we want to come down, we walk along the beams and jump onto the hay pile over in the far corner. This is great fun (if you don't have a dislocated shoulder).

Now, as I write on this grubby piece of paper, I'm up on the old beams. The planks aren't as bad as they first looked and I've nudged three together so it feels as if I'm on a kind of aerial raft. Mrs Froyland has given us blankets and a chamber pot – and I've also carried up a little jug of water, half a loaf of bread and a bag of wizened old apples to keep us going.

I get the idea that we aren't the first people to have slept in this barn. But I haven't asked the Froylands and I'm sure they wouldn't tell me. There seems to be a certain etiquette to being a hideaway.

Åse Jeffries

8TH JANUARY 1943

I was frightened that I would just roll off the planks in my sleep. But I shouldn't have worried because …

I didn't sleep! For hours I lay looking up at the holes in the barn roof, feeling the plank digging into every possible hard bit of my body. Other people count sheep, but last night I counted the knobbles on my spine. I'm now personally acquainted with every single vertebra and small bone: they all wanted to say hello.

And then I completely forgot how uncomfortable I was because I heard footsteps. Heavy footsteps. There were men's voices, talking loudly in German.

The soldiers tramped into the barn, swinging torches. I was on my side and I quickly shut my eyes. I felt that if I looked at them they might get that prickly feeling at the back of their necks that someone was watching them. So I lay there with my eyes screwed up and my body frozen with fear. I hadn't even had time to wake Fred so I just had to pray that he stayed still and didn't make a noise.

The Germans went on stamping up and down, joking and laughing about some drinking competition they were planning for when they went off duty. I peeked a look. Two of the soldiers were jabbing at the hay pile with their bayonets. I immediately shut my eyes again.

Then suddenly the voices were only coming from one place – the soldiers were directly under me, by the entrance to the barn. They stopped here and the conversation changed tone. Something serious was being discussed, though I couldn't make out the words. I screwed up my eyes even tighter.

At last I heard them leave. The voices and the plod of the boots started to recede. But they took their time – it seemed ages before they were entirely out of earshot and I could breathe again.

Fred, of course, had slept through everything!

Later – I think a couple of hours had gone by – I heard boots approaching the barn again. I froze. This time the tread was more purposeful. This person knew exactly what he was doing.

I heard the ladder being dragged across the barn floor. The poison capsule was in my coat pocket – there was no time to get it now.

Someone was mounting the ladder.

I fumbled in my sleeping bag. There's nothing like a nice warm, weighty gun in your hand... I released the safety catch and waited.

I gave Fred a nudge. He made a chewing motion and snuffled back into his sleeping bag. Well, he'd wake up soon enough.

The Colonel had taught us to aim for the centre of the chest, but now I needed the element of surprise. I'd have to take a risk and skim the top off this German's head as he came up between the rafters.

It was me or him. I aimed the pistol, my arm quivering.

Then the creaking stopped. There was a little cough and a man said, "Åse? Are you awake?"

It was Haakon.

"Ah, hello," I said, as casually as I could. I thought it best not to let on that I'd been about to blow his brains out.

Haakon came up the last few steps of the ladder and I shone the torch at him. He was fully dressed, but heck, did he look a fright! His hair was tangled and matted and there were stains all down his shirt front. His hands were dark and so too were his wrists and forearms. Haakon seemed such a gentle soul. But he'd clearly been up to his elbows in blood!

"What happened!" I cried. "What did you do to them?"

"Who?" said Haakon.

"The soldiers!"

For a second he seemed puzzled, then he looked down at his hands and laughed.

"It's only beetroot juice."

"Ah!" And I laughed too.

Haakon crawled across the beams and sat down on our little raft. He seemed to have forgotten about Fred's shoulder, for he gave him a vigorous shake. Fred let out a great groan of pain, opened his eyes and looked around him blearily. He didn't seem a bit surprised to see a huge, wild-looking man completely kippered in beetroot juice.

"It's not safe for you to stay here," Haakon said. "The Germans are clearly on to something. Get your stuff together. It'll be dawn in an hour and we want to be on the road by then. I've got a lorry ready – you're going in under the beetroot."

"Can't we just hide in a hay lorry?" I asked. "It'd be a bit more comfortable."

"Beets are better," replied Haakon. "Germans won't touch them – they hate getting stains on their uniforms. Anyway, by the time you get to Sweden you'll look back on the beet lorry as luxury!"

This didn't sound too good. But sometimes it's best *not* to know what's in store. So I purposely didn't ask Haakon "Why?" or "What happens next?". And I silently prayed that Fred wouldn't ask either.

"Why?" asked Fred.

Haakon dropped his voice. "I'm afraid you're to go into the gutting bins at Tønsberg harbour."

"Gutting bins," I repeated tonelessly.

"That's right," said Haakon. "We've a boat lined up to take you to Sweden. But while you wait in the harbour, the bins are the only place smelly enough to put off the sniffer dogs."

So that is what awaits us: gutting bins, followed no doubt by a rough crossing hidden away in the hold of some tiny fishing boat.
I suppose nothing will make any difference now. Fred and I are scratched and smelly and worn to the bone. And after all that's happened, a few old fish heads can hardly hurt us now.

Jakob P. Stromsheim

15TH JANUARY 1943

I haven't filled in the diary for eight days. It's partly because we've been so tired and partly because we've been sleeping rough (this is the first night that I haven't felt the wind on my back). Also, there has been so little to say. All we've done is travel on and on over vast, endless valleys and mountains, hoping all the time that we might be getting nearer to Sweden.

Everything here is white. The snow blurs any landmarks – it hides bogs and lakes and deep ravines. So every single valley looks the same and our map has become impossible to follow. We keep pushing east and trust to the stars, the sun and the strange little button compass.

But some things *have* changed.

A few days ago the mountains were much steeper, but now we're on lower ground with smaller hills and valleys. The nights have finally become a little less cold, but there are no huts. We've passed a few farmhouses, but we have no idea whether the local people are friendly or informants. When it gets dark we find a sheltered spot, eat our pemmican and raisins, stick our boots into our sleeping bags (frozen boots are just unwearable) and huddle up together for the night. The wind has blown constantly, but there haven't been any storms. And while we are never dry and we're never really warm, at least we aren't freezing.

I've got Lars to thank for that. He isn't exactly chatty – hours can pass without him even opening his mouth – but he does know so much about survival outdoors. He's shown me how to start a fire using the heartwood from the very middle of a pine tree where there's plenty of sap. And it was his idea to place brushwood under our sleeping bags to stop the melting snow from soaking us. He can judge distance, too, or tell if we're approaching running water. Also – and this is the strangest thing of all – he's got an animal's instincts for the weather.

This afternoon was a typical example.

We were skiing along as usual and suddenly, halfway down a hillside, he just stopped. I asked him what was wrong. He scowled up at this glassy blue sky and said, "There's a storm on its way."

I looked all around. It was true there was a nip to the wind, but there were no clouds and the snow was firm and hard underfoot. Conditions seemed pretty good.

But Lars's eyes were moving across the valley, looking carefully at the terrain. "Haven't you felt the wind?" he said. "It's in the east now and the smell of the air has changed."

I'd never thought of air as having a smell.

Lars pointed further down the valley to a shallow hollow in the hillside. He said, "That's a good spot over there. Come on. We haven't much time."

When we reached the hollow, the wind was already colder. I untied the juniper branches which I'd been carrying to use under our bedding and I started laying them out on the ground, but Lars handed me our spade.

"We won't survive the night out here," he said. "We've got to dig a hole."

"A hole?" I couldn't believe what I was hearing. Nobody in the whole world hates being in a hole as much as Lars. When we were on the assault courses at Drumincraig he'd do anything rather than crawl down the Colonel's drainpipes.

"Yes, a hole!" said Lars abruptly. He thrust both hands into the hillside and removed a great chunk of snow.

"How big?" I asked.

Lars took another armful of snow. He didn't look at me. He just gave a shudder and said, "About coffin-sized. Maybe a little bigger."

So Lars taught me the art of a good snow hole. The secret is to start low and then dig up into the hillside at an angle – that way it's easier to push the snow back out of the way. Also, since hot air rises, the doorway keeps out some of the cold.

After about half an hour of burrowing we had our snow hole – about a metre tall and just big enough for both of us to lie down flat. I spread my branches out on the floor of the hole and Lars pushed a ski through the roof a couple of times and swivelled it round to make air vents.

We crawled inside for the night and Lars propped a heavy sweater over the door with a couple of bits of wood. I lit a tiny stub of candle and we ate the very last of the pemmican. It was really quite cosy – in fact it was so warm that the walls and ceiling were melting slightly.

I suggested to Lars that maybe we should've built a snow hole earlier, but he shook his head. "I hate 'em," he said. "During the night the ceiling always sinks in towards you. Don't sleep on your back, or you'll wake with snow up your nose."

And with that, he turned over to go to sleep.

So that's where I am now – down a hole, lying on my stomach on a layer of branches with the log book in front of me. There's something quite animal-like about this hole – especially as our boots and sleeping bags are now pretty rank. I wonder what it looks like from outside. Would a passerby see a strange pale glow coming from the snow?

The candle is beginning to sputter and soon it'll

SPECIAL OPERATIONS EXECUTIVE

How to make a Snow Hole

HOW TO MAKE A SNOW HOLE

If you camp out overnight in the snow without a tent, you will be warmer inside a snow hole.

Exterior

1. Find a snowdrift that is sufficiently deep to tunnel a hole large enough to lie in. Take into account that the walls must be at least a foot thick and remember that the snow must be wet enough to be packable, but not slushy. If you cannot mould a snowball out of the snow then you will almost certainly not be able to make a snow hole.

2. Tunnel an entrance. Determine which way the wind is blowing and, using a shovel or spade, excavate your hole with the entrance facing away from the wind. Because hot air rises, make the entrance lower than the rest of the snow hole – and make a dip at the very entrance to trap cold air.

3. Burrow into the snowdrift, shovelling slightly uphill. The sleeping area should be about 30 cms higher than the entrance. Stop every few minutes to pack down the snow with the back of your shovel. The structure needs to be as strong and hard as possible. The hole does not need to be the height of an igloo – there should be enough room to crawl in and out and to lie down in (and place your pack inside). The headroom can be restricted – you do not need to be able to sit up properly.

4. Use a ski stick or a piece of wood to create two holes, several inches wide, in the roof. This will ventilate the hole and prevent the build up of too much moisture.

5. Smooth off the inside walls (to stop melting snow dripping onto your sleeping bag) and then, with a pocket knife, dig small grooves in the floor and on the walls of the cave to allow melt water to drain.

6. Outside, gather the snow dug out of the hole to build a windbreak in front of the entrance. Some of this spare snow can be packed onto the walls of the hole to improve insulation.

Interior

7. Mark the outside of the snow hole with some of your belongings so rescuers can find you. Before settling in for the night, make sure that the shovel is inside the hole in case you have to dig yourself out in the morning.

8. Snow is a good insulator but a poor mattress – layer some branches or matting between your sleeping bag and the ground.

NB You can burn a candle in a snow hole. But do not light fires – the build up of smoke could be dangerous and the heat may make the roof or walls of the hole cave in.

burn itself out. I'd better turn in now. Instead of counting sheep, I think I'll keep a tally of the drops of water falling from the ceiling – that should carry me off to sleep.

Jakob P. Stromsheim

16TH JANUARY 1943

We are still down the hole. We've had an extraordinary and dangerous night that has changed all things for ever and brought us close together. I find that every word that Lars has uttered still rings in my head.

This is how it all happened.

I woke in the very dead of night with the feeling that something wasn't right. I couldn't see anything, but I did have a certain "closed in" feeling and I put my hand up to touch the snow. Lars was right – the ceiling does shrink downwards.

There was no sound, no movement – just my breathing. This darkness was too quiet and the air too still… Then, suddenly, I knew exactly what was wrong: I couldn't hear Lars breathing.

I reached out to the other side of the hole. My hand came to rest on branches and hard-packed snow. My heart missed a beat. I reached out again. Lars had gone.

I wriggled out of my sleeping bag and thrust my boots on. There was barely room to move in the hole, so I had to crawl backwards along the passageway. I pushed away the sweater in the doorway and came out into a wild, moonless night.

A chill wind hit me in the face. I took a small torch from my pocket, and switched it on. Then, cupping my hands round my eyes, I tried to peer out. At first all I could see in the torchlight was whirling snow.

But then I caught sight of him. Lars was only a couple of metres from our snow hole and he was sitting propped against the hillside, facing directly into the wind. He's usually so careful about the cold, but now he had no hat on. His anorak was unbuttoned down to his midriff. One bare, white hand lay limp on his lap. His face was pale and his eyes were half-closed.

"Lars!" I cried.

Lars looked up at me and smiled vaguely.

"Lars! What are you doing?" I crouched down and picked up his hand. The flesh felt cold and hard. His face and hair were crusted with snow.

"It's the middle of the night! You're freezing!" I was screaming at him over the wind. "Where's your glove?"

He murmured something, but I couldn't hear him.

"Let's get you in." I grabbed his arm to hoist him up. But Lars was all limp and his legs wouldn't hold him. He staggered and gave a silly, careless laugh. I tried again and this time I held him round the middle and

half carried, half tugged him along. Lars was no help at all. I could see what the Colonel meant when he said hypothermia makes people act out of character. This wasn't the Lars I knew.

Somehow I got him back inside the snow hole, scrabbled around in my backpack, found the last three candle ends and lit them all.

Now I had to do everything I could to get him warm.

I took Lars's boots off and eased him into his sleeping bag. He wasn't even shivering, and that was a bad sign – it meant his body was no longer struggling to keep warm but had already begun the process of shutting down.

Lars normally hates being touched, but there was no other way to warm him. I unzipped the top part of my sleeping bag, took off my jumper and pressed my body against his freezing cold chest. He was too cold and sleepy even to flinch.

"Lars! Come on!" I gave him a shake. "Don't fall asleep!"

He gave a little grunt.

"Let's sing a song, Lars!" I cried. I was desperate – I *had* to keep him awake. So I sang. My voice sounded reedy and hoarse, but I kept going anyway. I sang "Ten Green Bottles". Then I tried "All Things Bright and Beautiful", but that somehow sounded ridiculous here. So I thought of something Christmassy and moved on to "Hark the Herald Angels Sing."

But Lars was not rousing. In fact his breathing was becoming heavier. As I sang, I tapped out the rhythm on his shoulder and rocked him vigorously to and fro. If he fell asleep that would be the end.

"Come on. Can't you feel you're getting warmer! Don't give up!" I cried. I shook him good and hard, partly because I was angry. "Why'd you do it, Lars?" I gave him another sharp shake. "Why did you go out like that?"

Lars's right eye opened just a slit.

"Couldn't stay inside," he murmured.

"But it's mad to go out in a blizzard! You of all people should know that!"

"I have this dream." Lars closed his eye again. He took a big breath, as if gathering his strength. I waited.

When he did eventually begin to speak he sounded more awake. "I've had it before," he said. "I think I dream it every night. It won't go away."

"What is this dream?" I asked.

"Oh, it's the same every time," he said wearily. "I'm buried alive. I'm lying in the darkness all tied up – earth all around me, no air, and I can't get out."

"So that's what happened tonight?"

"Well, it was worse, wasn't it? I woke up and I *was* buried in a hole. I was in this horrible snowy grave. I had to get out. I can't remember what happened after that."

"You took off your glove, that's what!" I replied. "Give me your hand now, Lars. I need to warm it up."

"No point," said Lars. "It's gone."

"Rubbish!" I pulled his right arm out of the sleeping bag. Lars didn't resist. He just lay there with his eyes closed, while I held his frozen hand up close to my mouth and breathed on it.

The fingers were waxy and white, and the nails bluish. I didn't want to look too closely because his hand felt like a dead thing. And Lars was possibly right. He might lose his hand – there were two fingers that felt very hard indeed.

I realized that warm breath wasn't going to be enough. I undid my shirt jacket and put Lars's hand under my armpit and squeezed hard with my arm. It felt as if I was hugging a shard of ice.

Lars's eyes were open now – open, but not seeing. His mind seemed far away.

I watched him carefully. Maybe now, after all these weeks together, it was finally time to talk.

"Lars?" I asked tentatively. "This dream, what's it about?"

Lars took a deep breath and then, fixing his gaze on the snow above him, he began speaking in a low, level voice.

"Just before I came to Scotland, I was living with my uncle by the coast, near Egersund, to the south of Stavanger. One afternoon I was out in the woods. My cover, if I was caught, was that I was hunting squirrels. But in fact I was doing a bit of reconnaissance – we knew that a German patrol had been in the area that morning and I was sent along to see if they'd been up to anything. I hadn't gone far – I was only about a hundred metres from the road – when I came to a small clearing where a long, deep trench had been freshly dug.

"I couldn't work out what the trench was for. Now,

looking back on it, I'm amazed I didn't guess. We'd had plenty of experience of the Gestapo. And we were only a few kilometres from the prison camp at Slettebø.

"In any case, I was standing there trying to work it all out when a lorry drew up at the side of the road. Then I heard footsteps. I ran to the far side of a mound a few metres away and ducked down behind some undergrowth."

Lars's voice was getting stronger.

"Along came this German patrol with a line of British soldiers dressed in army uniform, though some were only half-dressed, and had blankets wrapped round their shoulders, as if they'd been pulled out of bed.

"They were in a terrible state, filthy and bloody and bruised and ill-looking. They'd clearly been brought here in a hurry. Some didn't even have shoes on or belts and were holding up their trousers. Some were wounded and couldn't walk properly – they stumbled along, and if they got too slow the Germans would prod them with their bayonets.

"When they came to the clearing one of the Germans shouted something and the prisoners huddled into a ragged kind of line. With the trench in front of them, they must have known what was going to happen, yet they still formed a queue. I suppose that's Englishmen for you – they'll queue for anything, even death."

Lars gave an ugly little half-choked laugh, then he went on.

"The soldiers grabbed the first prisoner in the line and stood him up by this huge maple tree. The commander shouted 'Achtung!' and they shot him. Then two soldiers dragged his body by the legs and flung it to the side.

"Then they moved on to the next prisoner and did exactly the same. Then the next man, and the next man, and the next. Again and again and again. And each time the pile of bodies beside the ditch grew and the queue shuffled forward a little more. The prisoners were so crushed and resigned. Nobody tried to escape, and nobody talked. I saw one prisoner fingering a rosary and another looking up at the sky for a long time. But mostly they just huddled along, shivering. A couple of the men had dark patches on their trousers where they'd wet themselves.

There was one poor fellow I'll never forget. He crumpled to the ground before they'd fired any bullets into him. I don't know if they noticed because they hauled him on to the pile all the same.

"Then, when they'd finished shooting, they got to work on the pile of bodies, flinging them into the ditch one by one. Afterwards they took out a few shovels and, while the commander had a cigarette, the others filled in the ditch."

"Are you saying that they buried one of the men alive?" I whispered. I don't know why – nobody was going to hear us down in our little hole.

"Well, they were in a hurry, weren't they?" said Lars. "People are often in a hurry when they're doing evil things. I don't know how anyone could throw a warm body into a grave. But they didn't feel for pulses or anything like that. They just threw the bodies straight in."

Lars propped himself up a little, leaning on one elbow. "Because I was uphill from the clearing, I had a good view. I watched that pile of bodies and I saw one man blink. I'm sure of it. I looked at him and I think he looked at me. His eyes were so shocked – he thought he'd be dead, that the worst would be over, and of course it wasn't. Then he blinked again."

Two rivulets of tears ran down the sides of Lars's face into his hair. "So that's what I saw," he continued, "that man's eyes. And that's what I seem to see every time I open my own eyes. And every time I close them at night."

Lars lay very still for some time. Then he gave a sudden jerk and grimaced.

"Hey! You're squeezing my hand."

"No. I'm not," I said. "That must be the blood coming back into your fingers."

Lars screwed up his eyes. I'd read enough about frostbite to know that the pain would get worse. I took Lars's hand out from under my armpit and looked at it. Poor Lars. The fingers were still so white and hard.

"What happened next?" I asked.

"When the Germans left, I got up and I ran and I ran and I ran. I suppose, in a way, I've been running ever since. Uncle Rurik wanted to put me on a fishing boat to Scotland. He told my parents he thought it was best if I left. He didn't like the way I was behaving – I kept going back to those woods. I don't know why, but I couldn't keep away. The Germans caught me there one night and took me in for questioning. I don't want to tell you what that was like, but I'm sure the only reason they didn't kill me was because I was a kid. After that, Rurik said I *had* to go. I needed to get away and there was work to be done in Britain. He said the Germans might recapture me and interrogate me all over again.

"So I was stowed away on a boat and taken to the Shetlands. Sergeant Sneyd met me off the boat and brought me to Drumincraig…"

Lars's voice trailed away. After a while, I heard his

breathing change and realized he'd fallen asleep. This time I didn't try to wake him, for he no longer seemed to be in danger – it was just his fingers that were bad. So I sat there with his frozen hand still lodged in my armpit.

I felt fidgety and not at all in the mood to sleep. My mind kept returning to Lars's story: those prisoners and that ditch in the forest.

Then a terrible thought struck me. How slow-witted could I be? This wasn't the first time Lars had spoken of woods. This wasn't the first time he'd mentioned Egersund. When we got lost out on that reindeer hunt and he gave me Father's button compass he said he'd found it *in a wood near Egersund*!

I felt slightly sick and took several deep breaths. I simply couldn't afford to be ill or upset.

I shuffled round to face the other way and moved Lars's hand from one armpit to the other. His skin didn't feel quite so cold now.

Lars flinched. Then he opened his eyes. "My hand's burning," he said.

"Can you feel all the fingers?" I asked.

Under my arm, I felt his hand twitch.

"No. The little finger and third finger are numb."

This was not good news – those were the fingers that had felt hardest when I found him.

"At least it's not your foot," I said, trying to sound

cheerful. "Then you wouldn't be able to ski and we'd be lost."

But the burning sensation seemed to be getting worse. Lars's features were soon clenched with pain. His breath came in short, sharp bursts. I squeezed his hand all the tighter.

"I think I'm paying for what happened," said Lars.

"What do you mean?"

"That prisoner. I should have tried to save him."

"But what could you have done? There was a whole troop of German soldiers there," I say.

"I could've told someone," Lars replied. "We could've dug the grave up that night. But I didn't tell anyone. I was too frightened. I didn't have the courage to think it through."

"Lars." I paused. I didn't know for sure. Did I really want the answer? Well, I suppose I *had* to know the worst. I had to be sure.

"Lars, that little button compass you gave me? You said you found it in a wood near Egersund. Was it in *that wood*?"

Lars unscrewed his eyes for a minute and looked at me warily.

"Yes," he said. "The compass must have belonged to one of the prisoners. I found it lying in the mud just where they'd queued up."

So that was it. My father wasn't missing. He was dead. Mother always said we must assume the worst, but there was a mighty difference between assuming and knowing.

And now I knew. No Father, no long walks with him on the beach, no fishing trips, no cosy feeling at home at Christmas with the three of us together round the fire. I'll never hear his voice again, or see his smile. I can no longer save up stories to tell him. I can no longer hope.

Which of the prisoners was he? Most likely he was the prisoner looking up at the sky. He always was clear-headed. He'd have been thinking … and thinking fast. And he would have wanted to leave a message or a memento.

I turned back to Lars.

"I think he dropped that compass on purpose."

SOE | SPECIAL OPERATIONS EXECUTIVE

Hypothermia & Frostbite

HYPOTHERMIA

Hypothermia occurs when the core temperature of the body goes down to less than 35°C. A person suffering from hypothermia will start to shiver, their breathing will slow down and their speech will become slurred. Other symptoms are the skin turning cold and pale and a lack of coordination. Victims can become lethargic and confused (they can even start removing items of clothing). In severe cases, hypothermia causes muscle rigidity and irregular heartbeat. If untreated, victims will eventually lose consciousness and die.

When travelling in cold conditions, look out for the six **F**s of hypothermia:

FATIGUE, FITS OF SHIVERING, FOGGY SPEECH, FUNNY BEHAVIOUR, FALLING, FAINTING

TREATMENT

1. Find shelter and bring the casualty in from the cold.
2. Remove any wet or tight clothing and replace with warm, dry clothes, making sure you cover the head and neck.
3. Wrap the casualty in blankets and, if possible, have one or two people huddle round for additional warmth.

NOTES

As hypothermia progresses, shivering stops in order for the body to conserve energy. A victim of hypothermia who has stopped shivering may be getting worse rather than better. Severely hypothermic victims may get worse as they get warmer. Watch for signs of cardiac arrest.

FROSTBITE

Frostbite means that part of the body is frozen; the skin and the tissue immediately beneath have died. In more serious cases, the dead tissue goes deeper. The areas most susceptible to frostbite are fingers, feet, toes, ears and the nose.

Skin suffering from the effects of frostbite will look white or yellowish or purple. The flesh will be hard and probably numb. At this stage the frost-bitten areas will not be painful – although some victims feel a dull ache or a "pins and needles" sensation. Some people have walked miles to safety on frozen feet which made them stretcher cases when thawed. It is essential to escape from the cold before trying to treat frostbite – thawing and refreezing will almost certainly cause more damage.

TREATMENT

1. Find shelter. Warm the entire body and wrap the casualty in blankets.
2. Remove any wet or tight clothing.
3. Submerge the affected area in warm water (37.7 to 40.5°C). Do not use water above 42°C as this will damage the tissue. If warm water is not available, press the frostbitten area against warm human skin, such as a hand or chest or armpit. Do not rub the affected area – this may cause more damage.
4. Administer painkillers. As the frostbitten areas warm up, the victim will feel severe burning sensations and the skin may change colour and blister, or swell up. Apply dressings to the affected areas. If fingers or toes are affected, try to bandage them separately to prevent rubbing.
5. Give the victim fluids and food, especially carbohydrates and simple sugars that the body can turn into heat.

Fig 1: Frostbitten toes

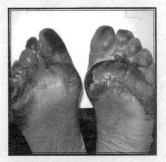

Jakob P. Stromsheim

17TH JANUARY 1943

The storm was over by
dawn and, when we
crawled out of the hole,
the valley was spookily
silent with a great pale
sun shimmering in the
sky. There was no sign
of Lars's right glove – by
now it had probably
been blown all the way
to Finland. So I cut
up part of a shirt and
wrapped strips of cloth
round his fingers. Then,
using two rather dank spare
socks, I improvized a new glove
(of sorts). But I didn't know if it
would do the trick, for Lars's hand looked terrible.
It was all puffy and the fingers still felt wooden. His
face also looked a fright – he was so gaunt and yellow.

I lit a fire and Lars huddled beside it. We were down
to just four raisins each for breakfast. We were weak and

cold and tired and lost in the snow and Lars needed a hospital for his hand. I felt panicky and close to tears, but I divided the raisins out, trying to give Lars the ever so slightly bigger ones (and this was ridiculous – how can you tell two raisins apart?).

Lars gulped down his raisins in one go (I nibbled mine one by one). "What about the syrup?" he said.

"The what?" I looked at him blankly.

"You know," Lars persisted. "The tin of syrup. The one with all the ants. It's in the top right-hand pocket of your backpack."

The syrup! I'd completely forgotten about it.

I took out the tin and prised the lid off with my combat knife. Inside the syrup was black and lumpy – almost more ants than syrup. We dipped our spoons in and as the syrup went into my mouth I shut my eyes.

The mixture was sweet and gritty. But at least the ants weren't moving. It wasn't so bad, just as long as I didn't think about what I was doing.

Quickly we finished the jar.

The syrup seemed to do the trick (or maybe it was the ants…). By the time we'd drunk some hot water and the sun had come up, we felt a bit better and were ready to set off.

We skied on through the morning, with me leading the way. I headed due east, with Father's button

compass tucked in my palm to keep me on course. I was feeling calmer now the turmoil of last night was behind me. And I saw that there was a certain symmetry to what was happening – my father too had been on a secret mission when he died, indeed he was most probably one of the operatives on that earlier attempt on Vemork. Maybe, in some form, he was with us now…

All morning we passed through small patches of pine and spruce. Then, just after midday, we climbed

to the ridge of a hill and saw before us what looked like a thick, dark wall of green. Hurrah! It looked like we'd reached the great forests that mark the border between Norway and Sweden. We were near to safety now. But how near? Thirty kilometres? Fifty kilometres? A hundred?

We came to a narrow path between the trees which led us down twists and turns until it dwindled into nothing, and left us tangled up among branches. We took our skis off and pushed on, sometimes walking backwards through thickets. But Lars was struggling. He stopped every dozen steps to lean on a tree trunk until he had recovered enough strength to go on again.

Further into the forest, we came to taller, older trees and the way became easier. For a few kilometres we followed the course of a small stream.

At last we arrived at the edge of a wide clearing, with some cows in a field, a couple of goats tethered up on a hillock and two small plots of cabbages. In the middle of the clearing, some 100 metres away, was a small cottage with red walls.

There were trim lace curtains in the windows and

a little line of smoke snaked up from the chimney. It looked very cosy.

"Let's knock on the door," I said, moving towards the open ground.

Lars grabbed my arm. "No!" he said, half gasping, half whispering. "It's not safe!"

I took a breath. It was madness to go on any further with Lars barely able to walk. I looked longingly at the little cottage and…

Aha! I screwed up my eyes, and looked more closely … YES! I felt a surge of relief and I turned to Lars with a huge, idiotic grin all over my face.

"Lars! We're in Sweden!"

"How d'you know?" He looked at me mistrustfully.

And it was wonderful, just for once, to be able to teach Lars something.

"Two things. Firstly, no Norwegian ever paints their house red."

"Hmm." Lars wiped his nose on his sleeve.

"And," I added, "what's your eyesight like?"

"It's good, you know that," said Lars.

"Well," I said, "read that sign over there."

"*Stäng grinden*," read Lars. "What does that mean?"

His hand was clearly really bad now – Lars doesn't usually have to have things explained to him.

"I don't know what that means," I replied. "And

I don't care. It could say BEWARE OF THE BULL or CLOSE THE GATE or WE EAT BOYS FOR BREAKFAST. The point is *it's not in Norwegian.*"

Suddenly Lars burst into laughter. And so did I. We put our arms round each other and hugged, and as we did so, I thought to myself, *Things are changing – I never imagined Lars* could *laugh.*

"Hey, look!" exclaimed Lars.

At the door of the cottage stood an old man in a tweed jacket. He held a pail in one hand and was beckoning us towards him.

Two words came bounding into my mind.

Fresh milk.

And that's where I am now – sitting on the rag rug by the stove in Mr Lysen's kitchen. He's given me some milk and it's delicious and sweet and still warm from the cow. We've had some porridge, too, and I've helped him with his chores. Mr Lysen has bound Lars's hand in a cloth soaked in vinegar. Tomorrow, when we've rested, we'll visit the hospital. It feels so good to be warm and fed and to have someone looking after us for a change.

Jakob P. Stromsheim

We're here in Stockholm at last! It wasn't exactly hard to find Freddie's café. Thanks to Mr Lysen, we arrived in the city with a map, as well as a hearty packed lunch. And when we got off the train we found there were signposts on every corner and friendly pedestrians who stop and direct you. And though it gets dark early in the afternoon, there's no blackout – I keep having to remind myself that Sweden isn't at war.

And just as Freddie said, the café had a sign with a little red cat hanging outside.

I pushed open the heavy swing doors. The interior was faded and old-fashioned with padded red leather seats and a dusty chandelier. There were no other customers except a courting couple and a man sitting in the far corner behind a newspaper.

We took a table by the window. I opened the menu for both of us because Lars's right hand was still wrapped in bandages.

"What'll you have, Lars? Smoked reindeer?"

Lars smiled and shook his head.

"Never again. You might just as well ask me if I want some moss. Let's have the pickled eel – I've been longing for pickled eel for months."

Well, there's no accounting for taste. I ordered and the waitress returned with two apple juices, a fruit tart (for me) and Lars's plate of pickled eel.

Lars ate clumsily with the fork in his left hand, while I gazed out of the window. In the distance, I saw two figures approaching – one tall and gangly, the other much smaller. The taller figure stopped and stooped down to examine something in the window of a bookshop. The smaller figure tugged at the tall one, forcing him to start walking again.

A minute later, Åse pushed open the swing door. She spread out her arms.

"At last!" she cried.

And we all hugged. Even Lars, after a tiny hesitation, joined in.

Åse noticed Lars's bandaged hand.

"What happened?" she asked.

"Just a bit of frostbite. The hospital says it's too early to tell. I may lose a few fingers, but it could've been worse," replied Lars.

"Oh! Can I have a look?" said Freddie. "I'm really interested in putrefaction."

"Shut up, Fred," said Åse quickly, and Freddie gave a little shrug.

We sat down and I was surprised to find I felt

slightly shy after all our time apart. After everything that's happened, I didn't know where to start.

Åse broke the silence.

"Nice seats," she said, patting the padded leather. "Fred, it reminds me of being in that Bentley with Mr Higgins."

"What Bentley?" I asked.

"Oh, we were picked up at Göteborg by this nice fellow from the embassy who brought us to Stockholm," said Åse casually. And as she spoke she moved the pickled eel plate to the other side of the table.

"Are you telling me that you were *chauffeured* across Sweden!" I couldn't believe what I was hearing. After all that Lars and I had been through, this just wasn't fair!

"Well, the rest of the journey wasn't that easy," protested Freddie. "My shoulder got put out again and they put it back without any anaesthetic."

And he too, just like Åse, pushed the eel plate away.

"Won't you try the eel?" I asked. Lars had saved a couple of bits for them. "It's delicious."

Freddie and Åse both made faces.

"We're off fish," said Freddie.

"I can't believe you'd ever be 'off' any kind of food, Freddie," I said.

And then they explained. They talked, for ever

interrupting and correcting each other, about their escape. At Tønsberg harbour they had crouched in the dark in these huge vats full of old fish waste and slime, and they had heard the German soldiers walking up and down the harbour inspecting the boats. Then, after hours and hours, night fell and a fisherman helped them out of the vats and brought them to the tiny hold of his boat. A minute later he slammed closed the hatch and they were trapped again in the dark for a long and rough crossing to Sweden. They both got seasick and huddled there all cooped up with the bits of old fish around them, feeling so ill and wet and cold and miserable that they wanted to die.

When they finished their story, Åse turned to Lars and said, "You'd have hated it down in that hold, Lars! There was barely any air."

"I'm through with that," replied Lars purposefully.

Åse looked at him very closely. And Lars, who kept his eyes fixed on the table all the time, explained. He didn't tell them everything, but he did describe the time in the forest when he watched the German executions. He also mentioned the nightmares he's suffered and how everything seemed to come to a head in that snow hole in the storm. Ever since that night, he said, his memories were just as clear, just as vivid, but somehow they hurt less. Things had altered and he didn't know quite how or why.

At this point Lars shifted his gaze to his bandaged hand and smiled a little sadly. "I feel better now," he said, "and if the price for that is losing a few fingers, I really don't mind."

Finally it was my turn. I dug in my pocket and brought out the little button compass, which was now looking even more dented and battered than ever.

I turned it over and showed Åse and Freddie the initials scratched on the back. I explained how it was my father's compass, and how, by a miracle of chance and fate, Lars had found it in that terrible wood all those months ago and had eventually given it to me.

"Now I know the worst," I said. "I know how he died. But I do get some comfort from this little compass that has got us over the mountains and into Sweden. Without it we would've been lost." I stopped and glanced round – I knew what I had to say next would sound strange. "I feel it's brought us good luck. It's almost as if someone's been watching over us."

"And there's somebody else who's been watching over us too," said Åse quietly. She nodded towards the corner of the café.

The man in the corner had put down his newspaper.

Sitting there, dressed in a big loose raincoat, was none other than Colonel Armstrong!

He beckoned to us with a finger and we all dutifully trooped over to his table. It may seem ridiculous, but I felt nervous. In a flash, all those weeks surviving up on the Hardanger, the raid, the escape into Sweden and everything else that had happened seemed to vanish from my mind. I felt as if I was back at Drumincraig, just about to be told off for doing something wrong.

"Take a seat," said the Colonel briskly. "Miss Jeffries, you're looking very thin. Won't need a lock pick now, will you? You'll be able to squeeze through the keyhole yourself."

Åse grinned. The Colonel lifted one eyebrow, then gave a little cough and continued.

"Now," he said briskly. "You've done well to survive. Nine out of ten. Not ten out of ten because I'm sure plenty of things went wrong up on the mountains that shouldn't have. Examine your consciences. Did you do well? Have you improved your levels of mental stamina? Your endurance?" He scowled at each of us in turn.

And, as his eyes raked over us, I thought to myself, *Colonel, you get ten out of ten for being a curmudgeon.* Is he never happy? If I won a battle single-handed against a hundred axe-bearing Samurai he'd still be dissatisfied. If I got ninety-eight per cent in an exam he'd say, "What about the other two per cent?"

The Colonel looked down at his hands and, as usual, they were bright red with cold. He cracked his knuckles. It was a horrible noise and I tried not to flinch. "But as for today, you're a right bunch of numbskulls!"

"Sir?" I said.

"When you came blundering in here, did you look around you? Of course you didn't! I was reading *The Times*, so you should have known I wasn't Swedish. Nought out of ten for observation. Don't you think it might have been wise to check up on who I might be before you all started pouring your hearts out?"

The Colonel sighed and cracked his knuckles again for emphasis. "It all goes to show," he concluded, "that you need more training."

"More training?" said Åse in a faltering voice.

"You'll have a little rest first and, heaven knows why, but your families may want a quick glimpse of you too. But we'll be needing at least a couple of you back soon. Mrs Collins will want to fatten you up like lambs for the slaughter. Also, I have this little project."

He shot us one of his graveyard smiles.

"And I have no doubt that you will all be volunteering!"

END NOTE

This story is based on fact. Jakob, Åse, Freddie and Lars are entirely fictional, but during the winter of 1942–3 the Allies did secretly send in Norwegian saboteurs to blow up the heavy water supplies at the Vemork plant up in the Hardanger Plateau. This turned out to be one of the most astonishing feats of bravery and endurance by any soldiers during World War II. Thankfully, no one was killed in the attack and, as this book goes to print, some of the saboteurs are still alive today.

Other things have also survived. The spectacles that the Vemork workman mislaid among his papers have been perfectly preserved and can be seen today at the industrial museum in Rjukan. The supplies that were dropped at the parachute jump really were in coffin shaped boxes and the telegram which mentions three pink elephants is also a true fact. Meanwhile, the Imperial War Museum in London has button compasses dating from the Second World War. Sadly all the SOE exploding rats have vanished.